MY CONTACT . . .

My contact took another document out of the briefcase. This one was gray with a bright red cover sheet stamped TOP SECRET. The title said *Minuteman Base Location and Configuration*. There were more documents in the briefcase.

"That's what you're selling," Shearing told me. "Oh, it's authentic all right. They already have it, but they don't know we know that. I don't mind giving it to them again, their local man won't know they have it. Of course, you wouldn't want the FBI to see you hand it over. . . ."

"But they're in on this, aren't they?"

Shearing grinned. "Not all of them. This has to look good, Paul."

"Look, if I get caught at this. . . . "

"We'll bail you out," Shearing said heartily. "But don't say a word. Just wait for us."

"Wait about twenty years," I grunted.

JERRY POURNELLE

RED DRAGON

CHARTER BOOKS, NEW YORK

Red Dragon was previously
published under the pseudonym of
Wade Curtis.

This Charter Book contains the complete
text of the original edition.
It has been completely reset in a typeface
designed for easy reading, and was printed
from new film.

RED DRAGON

A Charter Book/published by arrangement with
the author

PRINTING HISTORY
Berkley Medallion edition/May 1971
Charter edition/December 1985

ISBN: 0-441-71092-1

Charter Books are published by The Berkley Publishing Group,
200 Madison Avenue, New York, New York 10016.
PRINTED IN THE UNITED STATES OF AMERICA

To Poul Anderson, one of the Iron Men

1

I WOKE UP lying in the bilges with water sloshing over the floorboards. When I tried to get on my feet the boat took another lurch and threw me across the narrow cabin onto the chart table, squeezing water out of my clothes to drip on the Coast Pilot and charts secured there under their straps. A book fell off the shelf above me and clonked me a good one on the temple, and I grabbed it before it could swill around in the icy water at my feet.

The flashlight wasn't where it belonged, and I cursed, cursed again when I reached for my emergency light and it wasn't in place either. "Damn you, Steen!" I shouted, but he couldn't hear me. The wind was tearing through the rigging and in the little cabin it sounded like water was gurgling into the boat. I didn't think it was, but there was altogether too much water down there. Without a light I couldn't see if it was rising or not.

It was cold. Without my blankets around me I realized just how cold even before a gust blew through the open companionway, splattering me with sleet. As I reached for my boots the boat lurched again, throwing me into a sitting position on my

bunk. I grabbed the mast, holding on with my left
hand while I fished around under the bunk for my
sea boots. The right one was half full of water, and I
poured it out, cursing again but running out of
anything original to say.

Eventually I got my boots on, my feet trying to
curl up into little balls of ice and escape the chilly
water around them. Now that I had rolled through
the bilge I was wet and cold. I got my ski parka
pulled on over the wool sweater I had worn to bed,
then put my arms through the frigid stiff sleeves of
my yellow slicker and fished the sou'wester out of the
pocket. The boat hadn't sunk yet, and I didn't feel
like going out on deck until I had at least enough gear
on to keep from freezing.

When I climbed up the ladder through the companionway, I got the full shock of the wind, driving
sleet and cold right through my slicker and four or
five layers of clothes under it. The sailboat was
heeled way over, her port rail under and water
rushing along the deck almost up to the cabin sides.
Back on the stern seat there was an apparition, a
drenched figure in blue oilskins, salt crust hanging
from his eyebrows and sleet spattered all across him,
grimly holding the tiller and murmuring something
like, "My God, stop it, please, stop it."

Up on deck it wasn't so bad except for the cold.
The boat was carrying too much sail, and the sleet
was thick enough so that I couldn't see more than a
few yards in the black night. There weren't any other
lights in sight, and our own running lights seemed to
be shining through fog, throwing pale red and green
beams a few feet into the weather before giving up. If
there was anybody fool enough to be out there he'd
never see us. We heeled way over as another gust of
nearly horizontal sleet spattered across the deck.

I figured the wind at about forty knots, nothing to

get excited about as long as we were careful, but the sea was much higher than it should have been for that wind. All around us were tall gray waves with creamy white breakers on top, maybe eight feet high but on no more than twenty-foot centers from crest to crest, a short choppy sea trying its best to break us in half.

"You all right?" I shouted.

"No." He looked up with an effort from the compass, seeing me for the first time, then struggled to pull his sleeve up to get a look at the luminous dial of his watch. "Yes! It is not time for you to relieve me, I have another hour yet."

"Yeah," I answered. "Look, Iron Man, we ought to get some sail off this boat. I told you to call me if it got any worse!"

He managed a grin, struggling for a second before he flashed it at me. I could just see his face two yards away. "You call this worse? This is a pleasant sail! But I think I am frozen to the tiller!"

I moved aft to sit beside him, put my hand on the oak bar. "I have her," I told him. "Get up and stomp your feet, get the circulation going. In fact, go below and see if you can make some tea. I could use a warmup before I get out on that foredeck." When he didn't move I shouted again, "I have her! That's an order, Dr. Hoorne."

"Yes, sir. Would the captain care for . . . oh, blast it, all right, thank you, I would like some relief, but I could have held her until my watch was over."

"Sure you could, but I wouldn't be able to sleep the way you let her fall off. Threw me right out of my bunk!" I tried a grin, but it wasn't a very good one. Four days of this, three hours on deck and three below, no possible relief and the need to be attentive to every change in weather, do all the navigation, worry about the boat . . . I told myself for about the thousandth time that I'd never again go shorthanded

on a long trip with a landsman. "What about the
tea?" I asked. "I can hold her steady if you can
manage the stove."

To prove me a liar the sea threw a cross wave at
me, a tidal eddy about six feet high riding at right
angles to the seas we were plunging into. It broke
against us and the boat heeled dangerously onto her
beam ends, throwing her cockpit coaming under for
a second. A couple of gallons of water slopped into
the cockpit, sloshed around there while the little
scuppers slowly drained it overboard. That reminded
me, and I shouted again. "Where's the flash? Check
the level of water in the cabin, we must be taking in
some through the forehatch." In our haste to get
away from Seattle I hadn't checked everything, and
the forehatch couldn't be battened down tight
enough, so that every time a wave broke across the
foredeck—about three times a minute—there would
be a trickle down onto the double berth in the
forepeak, wetting the spare sails and soaking my
partner's seabag because he hadn't thought to put a
plastic bag inside the canvas. We weren't shipping
enough through there to sink us, but I wanted to be
sure that was the only source.

"I have lost one of the lights overboard," he answered. "The other is here somewhere."

"Blast it!" I exploded. "How many times do I
have to tell you, the most important thing at night is
to have a light were I can lay my hand on it instantly!
What if we were running on the rocks and I had to
find out where we were?"

"I'm looking," he told me. "Ah, here it is." A
sickly light bounced across the deck.

"Not in my eyes, I have to see the compass and
sails," I reminded him, trying to make my tone a little less unfriendly. "Fine, check the water level and
see if you can operate the stove. Better pump a few
strokes too, it'll warm you up."

He clambered below, lurching heavily against the cabin side. "Damn!" he shouted.

"Not again?" I said despairingly.

"Yes. Oh, I got it, the chimney didn't break."

"Good." The kerosene lamp over the stove was mounted a good eighteen inches outboard of the companionway, but somehow he managed to knock it off its gimbals every time he went below in the dark. After a few minutes he got it assembled and lit, and a warm yellow light flooded out of the cabin. It was too bright, but I didn't say anything. If it helped him get the stove operating, it was worth it. I wasn't thinking any too clearly, and a cup of tea would warm me up and get the cerebral action going again.

I shook the sleet out of my eyes and stared at the compass. Our course was south by west magnetic, which meant we were going a bit south of true west, beating our way up the Straits of Juan de Fuca from Seattle to the Pacific Ocean. I made sure of the time, decided it would be another couple of hours before we'd get anywhere near the shore. Ahead of us the Olympic Peninsula, Clallam Bay about dead ahead if my navigation wasn't too much off. Off to the right somewhere was Vancouver Island, part of the Canadian province of British Columbia, but we hadn't seen much of it this trip except for the tall striped spire of Race Rocks Light. On my last watch I'd driven the little cutter across the Straits as far as I dared, to within a few miles of the unlighted coast of Vancouver Island, so that I could turn in without worrying about navigation. The wind was steady, northwest by a half north, and all Hoorne had to do was keep her close-hauled on the starboard tack, giving us right of way over anything that happened to see us, not that boats in the Straits kept too good a watch. It was a risk, but not so much of one as keeping closer to land when there wasn't any visibility.

It took him a while, but he got the tea made, two

cups of absolutely boiling Earl Grey laced with honey and rum, something to chase the sleet away and warm us up from the inside. I may have drunk something in my life that tasted as good, but I couldn't remember it.

"You better get below and get some rest," I told him.

"You said we should take some sail in," he reminded me.

"We don't really have to. She's holding up pretty well." At sunset I had tucked a reef in the mainsail, set the small staysail and no jib, giving us a snug rig. "It isn't the wind so much as the sea anyway, and there's not enough to do anything but make us miserable. The danger in here is running into something hard." Such as a log, but it was early in the year for loggers. That was one consolation, anyway.

"Will it be this bad all the way to Los Angeles?" he said.

"Discouraged?"

"A little. Will it?"

"No and yes. Out at sea the wind ought to be behind us so we don't have to plow into it, and the seas won't be so steep without a lot more wind. This channel builds seas in here, some say this is one of the worst places in the world to sail." I didn't tell him that the Washington-Oregon coast was another contender for that title. He'd find that out when we rounded Tattoosh Island.

"You are sure you need no more help?"

"No, get below," I told him. I glanced at my watch. "Dawn in a couple of hours anyway. We ought to make Neah Bay tomorrow afternoon, we'll put in there and rest up before we take the big jump down the coast."

The rest of the night was pure hell. It had no business sleeting in mid-April, but it kept up all night anyway, and when morning came there was fog so that I still didn't know where we were. I kept the boat tacking back and forth across the channel, never sighting land, until about noon the fog burned away and we had a real horizon. There wasn't a thing in sight but an ocean liner way off ahead of us, her masts and hull just visible. A jet whistled overhead, bound for Japan.

"Are we lost?" Steen asked. When I laughed, he shouted at me. "Paul, I mean it, are we lost?"

"Of course not."

"Then why don't we see some land? This is a narrow channel, we should see land!"

"It's a twenty-mile-wide channel and we must be in the middle of it. Now go get us something to eat and stop complaining. I told you it would be rough out here this time of year." I leaned back against the high coaming, letting the sun try to dry me off. It wasn't doing too good a job of it. Two small cuts on my hands were white abcesses from the constant soaking in salt water, and the cracks around my finger joints were already open sores despite the cold cream I had rubbed into them. Every time I adjusted a line I felt a stab of pain. We were both wet clear through, and even our spare clothes were damp. Still, it was reasonably warm now, the wind had dropped off to maybe twenty knots, and the seas were calm for the Straits. It wouldn't have been too bad if I'd had enough sleep.

It was about two in the afternoon when we spotted Waada Island dead ahead, just where it should have been by my deduced reckoning. It really wasn't all that good as navigation—I mean, with a compass and a steady wind how can you get lost in a strait twenty miles wide at the most? But it was good to see land, even if it wasn't very friendly.

We drew up on the island, a little pimple covered with low pine trees. All the way up to it there wasn't a thing in sight, just the rocky coast and the slate-gray water. A surf broke, throwing foam fifty feet high against cathedral-sized rocks to leeward. When we got close to Waada the boat took on a different motion, a great swooping.

"Feel that?" I asked. "Real Pacific swells, not the chop we get in Juan de Fuca's territory. That's what we get from here south, you might as well get used to it." I stood, looked around the horizon ahead of us. "See—off the starboard bow, all the way out. . . ."

"There's nothing to see," he told me.

"Exactly. There's nothing out that way but China. You sure you're able to go through with this?"

"Look, we've put in five days getting this far. But is it safe? This is a small boat, will it stand . . ."

I laughed. "This boat is thirty-four feet, built out of oak and mahogany and silicone bronze fastenings. Eric Hiscock took a thirty-foot sloop around the world with nobody aboard but his wife. Hell, there was a sixteen-year-old kid set out of L.A. alone, got around the world in a twenty-four-footer. The boat can take anything that ocean can give, the question is, can we?"

"We have to, don't we. . . . Are you putting into that port there?"

We were drawing up on Neah Bay fast now, sailing with the tide. The little village, no more than twenty houses and the cannery, looked like a city after the lonely straits. The wind shifted another point north, so that I could let the sheets off and stop pinching *Witch of Endor*, and she showed her appreciation by racing through the water, making a good six knots easily, a river of white foam boiling smoothly past. I'd shaken out the reef and set the jib hours ago.

"Yeah, I'm putting in. We're not in shape to keep going, neither one of us. We need some rest, a shave and a shower. Need some fresh water, too, but this isn't the place to get it. Mainly, though, I want to run our laundry through a washer and dryer." There was something sensuously wicked about the anticipation of warm dry clothes.

"But there are people there . . . won't the FBI be alerted? They are looking for me pretty hard, you know."

"If the Bureau's got a man out here on this god-forsaken Indian reservation," I told him, "they deserve to catch us. There's nothing in Neah Bay but a cannery, some fish boats, and a lot of Indians. Watch out for the Indians."

"Indians?" he laughed. "What do you mean, watch out?"

"Liquor. They're friendly, but they're not allowed to buy booze in Neah Bay." I burst into song, a verse from a hideously obscene ballad a friend and I had made up about sailing in the Straits of Juan the—uh, de Fuca. "You'll lay in Neah Bay, day by day, and you'll stink as you turn slowly old and gray, for the water there is awful, and the women are all squawful, and NOT EVEN BEER IS LAWFUL, damn their eyes . . . speaking of which, open me a can, will you?"

"Then what's the danger? Will they steal our beer?"

I laughed. "No. They'll talk you into going with them to Clallam to buy some. A drunken Indian driving an old truck on a half-finished dirt logging road, barreling along at fifty miles an hour . . . now that's dangerous. Give me a storm in old Juan's Straits every time."

Witch entered the protected bay, gliding over smooth water, the wind shifting aft more and more so that she tore across the water, the only sound a peaceful hiss after the wild thrum out in the Straits. "My God, this is great!" Steen shouted.

"For a Norwegian, you sure don't know much about sailing, do you? But you're right, this is great." It was, too, the contrast with plowing into the steep seas now that we were as steady as a train on rails. Ahead lay a hot shower, dry clothes, all courtesy of the Bay Fish Company which had been nice enough to extend its facilities to me in the past when I'd sailed up this far. Not very many people were damn fool enough to sail to Neah Bay once, certainly not twice . . . and it was just starting for me this time. Ahead we had a thousand miles of Pacific Ocean, the first half along a coast with no safe harbors at all for small boats.

We put in at the floating pier, tied alongside just behind a big Seattle fishing boat. The grim old squarehead skipper sat in back cutting bait, the gulls screaming and wheeling about, diving for scraps he threw overboard. "OK, partner," I told Steen. "The shower's right over there. Oh, I don't think I'd shave, were I you. They do get newspapers out here. And keep your watch cap pulled down low, huh? I'd hate to have some sharp-eyed skipper spot you after all this trouble. I'll just get things secure here and I'll be along."

He trudged off, weaving a bit as his brain kept trying to convince his reflexes that he wasn't on a moving deck any longer. I wasn't too steady myself. I got the last of the lines coiled, pumped the bilges, and out of habit straightened *Witch* up to be instantly ready for sea although there wasn't any real need for it. It wasn't as if we were anchored on an exposed shore; Neah Bay is a fully land-locked harbor, the only safe harbor for small craft along that coast. There are other harbors, La Push for example, but there's a bar across the entrance with big breakers, and even the fishing boats don't try to run in there during a storm.

When I finished I walked over to the old fisherman and we chatted for a few minutes. Like most of them, he was alone on his forty-five-foot boat. Some take their wives, and a few hire paid hands, but they like to work alone. I like fishing-boat skippers, they're some of the last of the really independent citizens in this country.

He admired *Witch*. She looked nice with her fresh paint and varnish, everything trim despite what we'd been through. He'd never been aboard a yacht before, so I showed him around *Witch* before accepting a big glass of rum and pineapple juice back on his boat. I drank half of it, thanked him, and asked about the weather. The old captain spat, tossed a fishtail to the gulls, and pointed across to the south shore of the bay where the Coast Guard keeps a small station. There was a red triangular flag flying, and I looked sheepish. I should have spotted it on the way in.

"Hoisted her about an hour ago," the captain said. "Figure about fifty knots of wind out there by morning. Just my luck, the rest of the fleet's down catching fish."

"Yeah. Thanks." I looked at the small craft warning and thought about what it meant. We didn't have any too much time to get to Los Angeles, and it looked like we'd have to put out into that. How, I thought, now just how in hell do I get myself into situations like this? But of course I already knew the answer.

2

IT WAS EARLY April and it was raining in Seattle, but
that wasn't my problem. Rain in Seattle isn't a problem, it's a condition. My problem was what to put on
my income tax form where it said "occupation."

Actually there wasn't much choice in the matter. I
filled in "consulting engineer," which was true as far
as my intentions were concerned but a lie in fact.
What made it a lie was the state of the engineering
business in Seattle. With Boeing on one of its
periodic layoffs there were five engineers looking for
every project, and while I'd been independent a lot
longer than most of them, the competition drove the
fees down to nothing. I couldn't be too mad at the
fee-cutters—anything was better than welfare from
their point of view—but it didn't leave much for me.

So, what with the competition and the slump in
building and the rest of it, my real income didn't
come from the engineering business at all. What
money I got, and it wasn't much, came from the CIA
and that's why I had no real choice about the occupation blank on the form. You don't write "semi-
employed spy" on a government form. Besides, the
checks came from a systems engineering company for

"professional services"; I couldn't prove they were from the Agency at all.

The semi-employment was my own fault. Harry Shearing and his local counterspies had made it clear that I could work a little harder for them if I wanted to. The problem was with me. I didn't like what they were doing. The CIA isn't supposed to be in the counterespionage business and has no domestic authority at all, at least not on paper, and I wanted no part of their work here. I knew they worked in the U.S. because I had got roped into a couple of their operations, and I'd found out that the FBI was willing to overlook some trampling on the Bureau's charter as long as it got results and the trampling didn't get out of hand.

So I was semi-employed, which meant I didn't have a current assignment but they owed me money to clean up debts from the last time I "cooperated" with the Agency. The main debt was *Witch of Endor*, the prettiest little thirty-four-foot cutter I'd ever seen. The Agency was making good on the promise to keep up the payments on her, but that didn't pay my rent. If I hadn't had a couple of good years before the slump I'd have been on welfare myself.

I got the income taxes done with no more fraud than most people use, drew myself a beer from the cooler monstrosity some super-salesman got to me with, and waited for the phone to ring. The mail had already come with its grim score: Bills 5, Checks and new projects 0, so there was no hope there. I wasn't really expecting the telephone either, but after you pay all that money for an ad in the Yellow Pages you can hope some fingers stumble over you as they walk their way through.

I was about to draw my second beer when the thing did ring, and it took some self-control to let it go a couple of times before I picked it up. "Crane Engineering, Paul Crane," I told it.

"Hi, Paul. Janie. You busy?"

"Not really." Not too busy for you, I thought. Janie Youngs was the reason I'd have had to put "semi-employed" instead of "retired spy" on the form if I'd been truthful. I was still taking her to parties where the left-wingers in Seattle hang out, not so often now as I had back when my great adventures were just over because she'd met some other creeps to squire her around and I didn't get to see her as much as I'd like to. That's the way it was supposed to work, but it didn't make me feel any better. With my ex-wife gone off crusading somewhere east—thank God—Janie was the only female around who'd give a damn if I dropped dead some rainy afternoon. I liked to think she'd miss Paul Crane and not the junior counter spy I hadn't turned out to be.

"I have to see you, Paul. Right now, can you come?"

"Where?" I glanced at my watch, a little after one. "There's nothing my answering machine can't take care of, but I'd hate to miss a client. Don't have any right now."

"I think," she said carefully, "we can take care of that problem. Meet me at the colonel's house as soon as you can get there."

"Yeah." That meant business, which was great, but it was a disappointment too. I thought it over for a second. "Sure, doll. I take it I'm supposed to come alone."

"You know how. Bye." The line went dead and I put the phone back on its cradle. I couldn't have asked her anything if she hadn't hung up, the first thing they taught me was never to trust a telephone.

On the way out I glanced over my collection of guns and wondered if I ought to carry one, which was just plain silly. If I'd needed to be armed she would have told me, and I was just being a romantic little boy instead of a presumably grown man nearly thirty. I made a face at myself in the hall mirror, switched the telephone to the recording gadget that was supposed to take all my calls "on the first ring, answers them in your voice," and went out to the garage cursing the device. It doesn't cost that much to have a real answering service, and I should have got one instead of the idiot machine. I know I hate to get a machine when I call somebody, and I wonder how many clients I've lost because of the mechanical wonder. Now if you just dared put on a different type of message—once, far too late in a tavern, a buddy of mine and I had constructed messages for the machine to deliver. "This iss a recording. In five seconds, you vill leave your name and address. If you do not, ve haff vays!"

Out in the garage I had two choices. My '66 Formula S Barracuda with about a hundred and fifty thousand miles on it, or the current reason for financial disaster, the almost new TR. There wasn't much choice, the top leaked on the Triumph—why in hell can't the British manage to have good workmanship to go with their brilliant engineering? I made another face at the sporty little TR and climbed into old reliable. She ran pretty good since the valve job I'd had done, but she needed new rings and I couldn't afford it. The tires weren't too good for wet weather, for that matter, which made me grade-one foul-up boy for the month; I had good radials with rain cleats on the TR, and the top leaked so I couldn't use it in wet weather. In Seattle, yet. You're doing all right, Crane. With genius like that, you're bound to go places.

The colonel lived up on Queen Anne Hill, across Lake Union from the university district where my old house sat smack in the path of a new commercial district. The house was doomed, the owner would get around to having it torn down one of these days. Everything seemed to be going wrong with Seattle,

leaving me down far enough for the rain to get to me.
When the rain starts to bother you, it's time to leave
the Pacific Northwest. The only problem was, where
in hell would I go?

The radio news wasn't any better. The Chinese
were again calling for a People's Revolution against
the Russian Fascists who keep power only with tanks
and armored cars and barbed wire, and the Russians
responded by calling Mao Tse-tung a philanderer and
not only that but he murdered his son in the Korean
War. The stock market was off ten points, the cost of
living was up somewhere near the top of Mount
Rainier, and unemployment was supposed to be
stabilizing at the highest levels in a decade. It was a
cheerful drive around Lake Union where they were
tearing out the last of a colony of fine old houseboats
to replace them with steel and glass high-rise apartments guaranteed to give a view of the polluted
water, but it was all right because the mayor had just
appointed the fourth commission to deal with the
lakes and this one was *sure* to do something.

Normally I like to drive. It's one thing I'm good at,
have been since I used to race sports cars when I was
a student at the University of Washington. My old
Barracuda might not be the most modern beast on
the road, but there wasn't much on the street that
handled better, and when properly tuned that big
high-compression V-8 is a lot more power than most
people realize. Today, though, it was just transportation. I took some corners pretty fast and wound up
side streets to the top of Queen Anne, making it impossible for anybody to follow me without being
seen. Nobody was, which didn't surprise me. There
wasn't any reason to be interested in Paul Crane,
unemployable engineer and semi-employed spy.

I don't really know who the colonel is. I've been to
his big brick house several times, the CIA people
seem to use it for conferences, but the colonel has

never been in on them. As usual he let me in himself, showed me to the door of his study, and went off somewhere. His limp was a bit more pronounced this time, maybe it was the wet weather. I bet myself there was a story about how he got it. Although I'd never talked to him more than two consecutive minutes, he struck me as the kind of guy who'd have a hell of a background and a closet full of medals he never showed anyone.

I wasn't surprised to find Harry Shearing in the study with Janie. I don't know what Shearing's title with the Agency is, but he's obviously the boss of the counterespionage operations along the West Coast. I'd only seen him in Seattle, but once when I tried to get him I was told he was in Utah, and another time in San Diego. For that matter, I don't even know where his main office is, although I've seen an office he works out of in downtown Seattle.

Shearing was sitting at the colonel's oriental rosewood desk, an ashtray full of dead Camels pushed off to one side, a cup of coffee dying on the other, and a sheet of paper covered with doodles in front of him. He didn't look six feet tall sitting there, but I knew he was; he's about an inch shorter than me. His dark blond hair was a little longer than the last time I'd seen him, like he was converting from the Prussian brushtop he usually wore to something he could comb.

Janie came over to meet me. With heels she was almost as tall as Shearing, a big stretched-out girl with straight blonde hair curling a little at the shoulders, the short plaid skirt showing about a yard of elegant legs that were no trouble to look at at all. She had her horn-rimmed glasses on, making her look like a bank loan officer, which she was, sometimes. The glasses made her look almost thirty, but I knew she was only twenty-five. They gave her a cold virginal look, and I knew better than that too. She took my arm, just a touch to guide me over to the third party in the room, but she had a way of touching me, not squeezing or anything describable, that made me want to respond if there'd been any way to do it. I was hoping that this conference would end with me seeing a lot of her.

"Paul, you've met Dr. Hoorne," she said positively. If she hadn't been so insistent about it, I would have said no, but as it was I took a closer look before putting out my hand.

"Hello, Steen," I said. I looked at him again, and it was Steen Hoorne all right. We'd been together at the university, but he was a graduate in physics while I was in engineering so we weren't close. A couple of times we'd gone over to the Blue Moon for beers after classes, usually with other fellow sufferers from Black Bart's course in technical writing, and I'd run into him at the goofy left-wing parties my ex-wife was forever dragging me to. He'd been just a guy I'd seen around, and I hadn't even seen him around for years.

"Hello. It seems that we are old friends, Paul," he answered. The slight accent I remembered was still there; Steen Hoorne grew up in the Ballard area where the whole population seems to be Scandinavian, and he'd learned Norwegian before he knew English. Not that he didn't speak English as well as any other American, but there was that little trace of an accent, just a suggestion, that got more pronounced after maybe the second pitcher of beer. "Old friends," he repeated, nodding significantly at Shearing.

"We are, huh?" I nodded, exaggerating it for sarcasm. "Thanks, Mr. Shearing."

"You're welcome," Shearing answered. "Have a seat, Paul. How's business?"

"Humph."

"That's what I like to hear. No new clients in the last couple of weeks?" Shearing looked at me intently as he said it, making me realize there was something important about the question.

"Nothing. Things are pretty tight just now."

"Good." He made it emphatic. "You're quite bitter about it, of course. So bitter that you're willing to sell secrets to the enemies of the United States, that is, provided you have any secrets to sell and you can find the buyers."

I sat in one of the colonel's oak and leather chairs, took out my pipe and made a production of cleaning it with my pocket knife. Hoorne took out a pipe of his own and messed about with it. Neither one of us said anything, but Shearing was good at waiting. He picked up his pencil and added a fortified wall to whatever it was he'd been doodling before, sipped at the cold coffee on his desk, lit another Camel. . . . "All right, Mr. Shearing, just what have you got in mind?" I asked. I was well aware that he'd scored a point by making me ask.

"Do you remember what Dr. Hoorne's specialty was, Paul?"

"Lasers, wasn't it? Little ruby red lights that melt holes in things. He was out at Boeing for a while when I was there, he worked in the labs."

"Lasers it is. Besides Boeing, Dr. Hoorne has been at Eglin Air Force Base, Aberdeen, White Sands and Holloman. . . . He's one of the best-known experts on the use of lasers for defense against ballistic missiles. Unfortunately the company he worked for didn't win the contract for that project, so he's been laid off. Terrible waste of a good scientist. Dr. Hoorne is bitter about the whole thing, aren't you, Steen?"

Steen spread his hands expressively. "It is a very disappointing thing, a man being unable to work in his own field." He chuckled. "At least we hope it can look that way. I am almost as bitter about it as you are, Paul."

I looked at both of them with a deliberately sour expression. It wasn't hard to see what they were driving at. "So just who's going to offer to buy our services?" I asked Shearing.

"The Chinese intelligence people, eventually," Shearing answered. "At least we sincerely hope so. Unfortunately, the best offer we have had up to now is from a free enterprise group."

"Eh? You better run it past again from the beginning," I said. I got the junk cleaned out of my pipe and started loading it. Steen was having trouble with his, so I passed my pocket knife over to him while I turned back to Shearing.

"From the beginning," Shearing nodded. "I want the Chinese intelligence net out here on the West Coast. The FBI hasn't been successful with it, and the people in Washington are upset because it seems that the Chinese very shortly expect to get their hands on some important information about our ballistic missile defenses."

"How do you know that?" I asked. The question marked me as a part-time agent, because the real pros know better.

"I can't tell you. The source is not in this country, and I've told you too much when I say that. Anyway, I've got permission to go after the West Coast Chinese net, and I've had Janie working on it through the contacts she's made in the university district. You have some strange friends, Paul."

"Yeah. Strange." He could call them strange. For my money, they were just dull. I don't know what all the modern rebels are like, but the bunch of losers my ex-wife had dragged me around with were a bore. They had only one conversation, what's wrong with the United States, and they played it over and over.

Oh, there were a few pretty nice guys in our old
bunch, but most of the good ones had long since
grown up and got out of that crowd. Nowadays the
ones who were left sympathized with the Chinese
against the Russians and sat around singing "The
East is Red," but that was probably because the real
Communist party wanted nothing to do with them.
"So she found a contact and you want Hoorne to
connect with him. Where do I come in? If I do, which
I doubt."

He ignored my last remark. "Not quite. What
Janie has run into is a group of disgusted unemployed scientists who seem to be willing to sell their
services to anybody who will buy them. They have
somehow managed to make contact with the Chinese
purchasing agents, but the only problem is that they
haven't anything important to sell to get them a
meeting with a top man." His eyes flickered over us,
rested on me. "You and Dr. Hoorne are going to fur-
nish them with a salable product."

3

"NOW JUST A blooming minute," I protested. "I see you coming. Look, you've made me bait for your anti-Chinese operations before and damned near got me drowned. Who tries to bump me off this time?"

"No one I know of, Paul," he said sympathetically. He had good control of his voice and if I hadn't known him better it might have had an effect. As it was, it reminded me of that cartoon cat who's always protesting his innocence. "All we want you to do is help establish Dr. Hoorne's authenticity. Not to mention helping keep Janie out of trouble."

"Sure. Bring her into it, too," I said. Boy, did he have me taped.

"I could use some help," Janie said. She looked right at me, not trying to turn on anything special, just asking for help, all blue eyes and blonde hair and an expression that said I could do anything if I'd just try.

"What kind of help?" I asked her, ignoring Shearing.

"With your ex-wife's record, it isn't hard to make you look like you hate the United States." Shearing didn't seem to notice that I was ignoring him. He never noticed anything he didn't like. "At least we can show that you don't care about espionage. And you have known Dr. Hoorne for a long time, they can check that easily, but it's very hard for them to find out you weren't close friends. You add a lot of authenticity to the setup."

"You need some authenticity, Steen?" I asked.

He looked up from his pipe, fiddled with the catch on my knife and finally passed it back still open. "It would help. Like you I went to the wild parties when I was in school, but unlike you I did not marry one of the local commissars."

"Now just a blooming—uh, look, Lois was a screwball, but she was no traitor. You're making it sound like she ran the CP or something."

"She did have some rather interesting friends," Shearing observed. "And luckily you are temperamentally the kind of man who never argues politics. So . . . we're not trying to convince anyone that you've been converted to communism, Paul, only that you're broke and hungry enough to sell to the highest bidder."

"Yeah. Make me a complete bastard. You can get up a little sympathy for an ideological convert, but . . . oh, all right, you don't need to give me the pep talk. I've got no use for Chinese spies, and I *am* broke. Just how does this work?"

Shearing took a file folder from a briefcase by the desk. "Here, this is a list of the times you've been out of town on projects. There's no way anybody can check on where you really went, and you don't make a habit of telling people, do you?"

I shook my head, and he went on. "So, we've changed your employers a little. You can hang on to this, just remember what's in it."

I looked over the list, discovering that I had been involved with the construction of missile bases for the last couple of years. It made sense, I might have been, although as it happened all my out-of-town projects had more to do with soil drainage and access roads than missiles. "OK, so what is all this supposed to mean?"

He took another document out of the briefcase. This one was gray with a bright red cover sheet stamped TOP SECRET. In small letters below it told me that "this document contains information affecting the national defense of the United States within the meaning of the espionage laws, transmission or revelation of which to unauthorized persons is punishable by law." It's the standard marking for a classified document, but I hadn't read it for a while. The title said *Minuteman Base Location and Configuration*. There were more documents in the briefcase.

"That's what you're selling," Shearing told me. "Oh, it's authentic all right. They already have it, but they don't know we know that. I don't mind giving it to them again, their local man won't know they have it. Of course, you wouldn't want the FBI to see you hand it over. . . ."

"Good lord! But they're in on this, aren't they?"

Shearing grinned. "Not all of them, that's for sure. This has to look good, Paul. There are amateurs in the free enterprise outfit, but the Chinese top people will be in this. Wait until you hear what we have in mind for Dr. Hoorne if you think yours is good."

"Yeah. Look, if I get caught at this. . . ."

"We'll bail you out," Shearing said heartily. "But don't say a word, just wait for us."

"Wait about twenty years," I grunted. I looked at Janie. Her I trusted, and I was glad she was listening to all this. Of course that's what Shearing thought of before he invited her. It wasn't that I didn't trust Shearing, he wouldn't go out of his way to shaft me, but when he was on the trail he sometimes tended to overlook the problems of the troops. I thought about getting out while I could, but Janie was still there and still looking pleased with me. Damn it, why is it that men have to put on the big brave act for girls? And why couldn't I find one who'd be impressed with my skill at hunting or something?

"All right. I've got this document for sale. Anything else?"

"A few other things. You'll get them before you go. Now let's turn to the rest of the program." Shearing was talking faster now, no pretense of consulting me about the project. Not that he was ever consulting me in the first place, but once I was roped in he could make with the orders. He had a way of explaining things to himself, thinking it through again on the spot even though he'd planned it before, that reminded me of a math professor I'd once had. He lit another Camel and plunged on.

"Dr. Hoorne is also in possession of information, information that is somewhat more important than yours," Shearing told us. "In fact, his is so important that his disappearance with certain documents has brought in the FBI who, after judicious consideration, will put out an all-points wanted bulletin on him. That will be in the papers tomorrow morning, by the way. We've had to work fast, Janie's contact seems to be going out of town and we can't be certain these people won't slip up and let the FBI get them before we spot their buyer. Besides, we need to locate the Chinese agent before they get the real information they're expecting."

"But—but," I protested, breaking in on his monologue, "aren't you working with the FBI on this? Hell, they want the Chinese more than they want these free enterprisers, don't they? They won't grab them."

"It would depend on what they wanted them for," Shearing said carefully. He traced another diagram on the scratch pad in front of him. "You must understand, Paul, this whole operation is intended to identify the Chinese contact. Under no circumstances must he be arrested, made suspicious, put out of action, interfered with . . . that's vital. In fact, if you have to, you are to protect him from the Bureau, the local police, or anyone else you do not know for certain is working for me. Is that clear?"

"It's clear, but I don't know why."

"You don't have to know why." His voice had an edge to it. "You do not need to know why, but you will remember it." He looked around at all of us, his face an intent mask. "All of you remember it. This is an identification only, and you will not interfere with the Chinese agent once he is found."

He caught himself, relaxed visibly, but the tension was still in his eyes. There was something he wasn't telling us, but there'd be no way in the world to find out what it was. "Not that I expect you to find the Chinese agent. We've got a lot of lines out, chances are one of the other operations will spot him first. But this one has one sure thing going for it. We might not get to the Chicom, but you will be contacted by the information brokers. The story Janie will tell them makes that absolutely certain. After that, you may or may not make contact with our real target, but if you do, it is extremely important that this works the way I want it to."

"Yes, sir. Find them but don't spook them. Protect them from the Bureau." I banged my pipe against the big cut-glass ashtray. It rang harder than I wanted it to. "Just how do I do that?"

"Oh, hell, you won't have to," Shearing said. "Look, I don't have a lot of time this afternoon. I'd like to turn this over to somebody else but temperamental people like you have to . . . anyway, look, let me run through it and you ask questions afterwards, OK?"

"OK." I'd worn his patience a little thin, and for no purpose. He wasn't telling anything he hadn't planned to give me. I wondered what it would be like to really have to work for that character instead of being a part-timer who could quit. I also wondered if I could keep my semipro standing after this. He must have heard me thinking.

"By the way, you'll be paid your standard consulting fee for this through Hefflinger Analysis Corporation. I hope you can collect it back from the other side, but you'll get your money."

"Thanks." Well, at least I'd make the payments on the TR without hitting my savings.

"Yes. Now. Tomorrow morning the papers will have a story on the possible defection of Dr. Hoorne, local Seattle boy known to be unhappy with the government about being laid off. It will say that he applied for positions at the universities, but because they have dropped their military research, the government would not allow him to continue the work he was doing. There will be hints that there were some questionable security aspects to his layoff. And he is wanted for questioning by the FBI."

I looked around at Hoorne, but he seemed to be taking it all right. "He's going to come to you for help. You will hide him, Janie will discover he is at your place. That's reasonable, she's been there often enough. She'll let the secret sellers know about Hoorne, they will approach him, and the two of you will dicker over the price. Dicker hard. Eventually Paul will turn over this document to them as a gesture of good faith. They'll be able to sell it for a reasonable price, nothing spectacular but they ought to get five thousand dollars for it. I'd say you ought to hold out for at least half that. Paul will have other documents, all for sale. You'll have established that you have genuine information for sale, and now you ask for really big money. Hoorne will make himself available to their source, will answer questions, accompany them to any location to assist them in gaining knowledge of his specialty. He is not interested in defecting and has no ideological love for them. The two of you are purely interested in money, and you are suspicious, afraid of being caught and afraid of being kidnapped by the enemy. You want to be sure that your information will be paid for, which means in the case of the important secrets, money in advance."

"I see," I told him. It was getting clearer by the minute. "The Chicoms aren't likely to give this amateur outfit that much dough on speculation, are they?"

"No. It would not be reasonable, you are asking for a lot of money, at least one hundred thousand dollars, cash, small unmarked bills. Hold out for more if possible. You can start with an asking price of a million and come down. There are not many people the Chinese trust with that kind of money."

Janie laughed. "Would you trust one of us with it?"

Shearing looked serious for a second, his eyes burning through the cloud of smoke around him. "I'd have less trouble finding you than they would, you know. Unless you wanted to defect to the Iron Curtain or the Rice Workers' Paradise . . . that would be punishment enough." He got his grin back. "But I am trusting you with that kind of money. You can't keep it all even if you collect it. I'll give you a bonus if you can help bankrupt them, though."

"Thanks," I told him. "Well, it sounds easy enough. The only real danger is from our side. The Bureau's not stupid, what if they catch Steen? They'll really be looking for him, you say."

"Oh, yes. As far as they're concerned he's a genuinely wanted man about to give vital secrets to the enemies of the United States. We can't trust every agent, the other side must have some people in the Bureau by now. That's one reason for you, Paul. Except for your story there's really no reason why Dr. Hoorne should come to you for help. You weren't actually good friends, and the Bureau will never think of you. I hope. Keep him out of sight, though; he's known in the district.''

"Yeah. Steen, how does this sit with you?" I asked.

"Fine. You're the boss, tell me what to do.''

"Me? Come on, you must be an old pro at this.''

He laughed. "No, I am a laser-beam warfare expert. A little out of date, perhaps, but stuffed full of secret information, it is my specialty.''

"Well for God's sake,'' I protested. "There's nothing but amateurs in this show. Including most especially me. Why don't you at least put one of your . . . oh.''

"Oh is right,'' Shearing agreed. "Just how long do you think it would take one of my agents to learn enough about lasers to keep these people happy? Remember, we want them to go away unsuspicious. If you actually make contact with the Chinese we will arrange an interruption before Steen gives away any real secrets, but it will be a most delicate interruption indeed. Well, are you happy with it?''

"How should I know?'' I asked. "He says I'm in charge. You mean Janie, don't you?''

"No.'' Janie answered before Shearing could say anything. "In the first place, I may be out of it as soon as you make contact with them. Secondly, I can't have you working under me. It wouldn't—well, it just wouldn't work, that's all.''

"What she means is that her emotional involvement with you is such that she can't give you orders on her own initiative,'' Shearing told us. "Sorry to discuss this out in the open but we better get it understood. Children, this is not a teen-age dating

game. One of these days, damn it, I'll manage to
recruit some agents like the ones in the books. The
hard cynical characters who never let human emo-
tions get in their way. Then I'll probably have them
shot because I can't control them. Right now, I have
to use what I've got, God help me." He grinned with
the last sentence to soften it a little, but I got the impression he could have used somebody a little less
temperamental than Janie and me. Of course, he
probably had people like that working another side
of the game. I thought about it, decided that Harry
Shearing must be a genius. He'd figured out how to
take people like me and get his job done.

A couple of hours later I drove Janie back to my
place. By arrangement the doorbell rang a few minutes after we got there, and a chap with a thick
leather attaché case was on the porch. He looked like
a tired salesman, which he might have been; there
were enough of them coming around lately. To anybody watching us he might even have been a prospec-
tive client with his rumpled brown suit and thin top-
coat. He wore rubbers, which wasn't altogether usual
in Seattle although newcomers to the city often try
them before deciding that if you live in a city where
it's always wet, you're a sucker to keep putting the
damn things on and then having to worry about them
when you get where you're going.

"Paul Crane?" he asked. I agreed it was me, and
he added, "Bill Dykeman, Consolidated Network
Engineering. Want a couple of hours of your time."

"Sure, come on in." I led him down the hall, past
the big sliding doors that connect to my living-room
office, around through to the dining room where he
was out of sight. He sat down and put the leather
case on the table, took out a couple of boxes that
looked like radios. "We have a complete line of op-
tical and electronic equipment for surveying, and we

were wondering if you'd test some of it," he said as he connected earphones to one of the boxes and put them on. In the other room Janie put a record, Beethoven's *Fifth*, on the stereo, turning it up but not very loud, and the guy fiddled with the box for about ten minutes. Every now and then he'd make another remark about the mythical surveying equipment he was demonstrating, and I'd make some appropriate response. When he finished he wandered around to my telephone, asked if he could use it, made a call and proceeded to take it apart while it was still off the hook. Then he carefully put it back together again.

"If there's anybody listening to you, he's using something so damn sophisticated that he *knows* you'll have a check made," he announced. "But after today you're on your own. I'll put plugs on the phone, you disconnect it when you want a conversation you're sure is private. A phone can be bugged to pick up any conversation in the room with it, remember that."

I nodded. I seemed to remember reading that somewhere anyway. "Now, Miss Youngs, you have your standard kit here?" he asked Janie. She indicated a little overnight bag she'd brought from the colonel's place. I was disappointed until I saw it was only half full of electronics and junk. Dykeman ignored the various feminine things, concentrating on little electronic gadgets. "Everything seems to be in order," he told us. "You can keep this receiver, I've shown you how it works. Now, if you'll excuse me, I have to catch an airplane. I'm due back home for dinner, which I'll never make. My wife is going to kill me one of these days." I showed him to the door, watched him trudge off down the street, his feet squishing in the pools on the sidewalk. As he turned the corner he sneezed.

"What a friendly chap," Janie grinned when I got

back in. "I'm glad Mr. Shearing arranged for him. For once we're just us, with nobody listening at all." She moved against me and I held her a long minute, remembering the lingerie in her overnight bag and wondering how to be delicate in making sure she'd stay.

"Yeah." I kept remembering something else. This out-of-town expert, this man who flew in so that there would be no way to connect me with a CIA type in case they had the local debugger spotted—this guy had to have been arranged for some time ago. Boy, did Shearing have me taped.

We couldn't go out. Shearing had made it clear that from the time Dykeman left the house was not to be unguarded. It only takes a couple of minutes to put a bug in, and if somebody did we wanted to know who. Janie and I were able to go over our plan, flattening out the rest of the details while I cooked dinner. I had enough red snapper and redfish in the house to make a New Orleans bouillabaisse, the real thing, not some newspaper recipe imitation. It takes hours of concentration to do it right, but the result is worth it. I put Janie to pounding herbs and rubbing them into the fish.

I liked to cook and a New Orleans bouillabaisse is something worth a lot of effort, but it was hard to keep my mind on spices and sauce. Every time I got close to her I felt like grabbing her, which is a perfectly good emotion but it ruins gourmet dishes. When we finally sat down to eat, I'd rather look at her than shovel it in. She caught some of my mood too, but she managed to put it away with the appropriate remarks. Girls don't always appreciate it if a man can cook better than they can.

After dinner we watched television for a while, an educational-station production of a play about the courtmartial of the officer who'd commanded

Andersonville prison camp in the Civil War. One of the lead actors was the guy who'd played an emotional and rather incompetent officer in the old *Star Trek* series, and despite all his efforts I expected to see him in fancy clothes carrying a ray gun.

"Paul? It's really all right, isn't it?" she asked when we turned the stupid box off.

"What's all right?"

"Getting you back on the job. I really needed your help . . . it wasn't just a trick of Mr. Shearing's." She moved closer to me on the couch.

Whatever I'd thought about it, the main thing was that she was back. "Sure, it's all right. We're not doing anything to be ashamed of, it's just—hell, I don't know, I like the rules to be followed. The government is to protect the citizens from . . . well, from underhanded government agents. At least that's what I learned in school."

"You mean from people like me."

"No. Not even people like Harry Shearing. But suppose we got a real son of a bitch in Shearing's job. Somebody who didn't care whether the people he played God with were innocent or guilty. If we have secret police one of these days that's going to happen. What do we do then?"

She shook her head sadly. "I don't know. But if we don't have people doing Mr. Shearing's job, there may not be any country at all. Remember what President Lincoln did? It wasn't very pretty, or very legal either." She took my hand, ran her finger across it. "But I'm glad we're working together again. I've missed you, you know."

I kissed her, a gentle little kiss like high school. "I missed you too." Then I looked at my watch. "It's late. Look, you'll have to go home alone if we're going to follow orders." I said it as naturally as I could, but it came out a little stiff.

She grinned. "Oh, I'd be scared. I think you ought

to walk me home, Paul, I wouldn't dare go out in the district at night alone."

With her training I'd pity the mugger who touched her, not to mention the .38 she was wearing somewhere. I said, "Gee, but I was told we couldn't leave the place unguarded until my friend gets here tomorrow. We could call a cab."

"But, good sir, what of the evil cab drivers who prey on defenseless young girls? Good heavens, I might get—what is his name, that amorous friend of yours who drives a cab?"

"Ron. You're right, even a small chance that he'd be your driver is big to take. Well, much as I hate to defy the orders of my superiors, there's nothing for it but to brave the storm with you . . ." I grinned and stood up.

"You character, aren't you even going to ask me?" She took off the horn-rims.

"Sure, sweetheart. Darling, will you st . . ." but I never finished the sentence. This time our kiss wasn't like high school. We found a way to follow instructions after all.

4

I WOKE UP alone, which wasn't unusual but there seemed to be something wrong. I looked around in a mild panic, saw her skirt carefully hung over a chair, and then I heard the pans clatter out in the kitchen. She was a big girl and she always ate a big breakfast, and about the only time I ever ate in the mornings was when she was there, which wasn't nearly often enough. I picked up lace panties which we hadn't had time to hang up properly and draped them on the chair, then went off to the bathroom to shave, losing a little of the morning fog. I glanced at my watch. Ye gods, eight A.M. I'd hoped they quit making hours at that time of day.

We sat at the old kitchen table and I thought about the hundreds of breakfasts I'd eaten with Lois. For at least half of them we couldn't stand each other. Janie was wearing one of my old robes, with her long bare legs making the thing look better than a Paris original.

"You know, I could get used to having you around in the mornings," I told her. "You even make pretty good coffee."

She gave me a funny look. "Last time a man said

that, I sued him for breach of promise. You better watch out, Mister.''

''Maybe I won't have to be sued.''

She looked at me again, her eyes soft. I couldn't tell if it was something special, or just what you feel after you spend the night making love. ''Anyway,'' she said, ''we never know where we're going to be. At least I don't.'' She glanced at her watch, began to hurry with her eggs, looking everywhere but at me.

''Well, you could drop the Agency bit, couldn't you? I mean, if you want a career, you've done all right at the bank. Or I could always find something with a salary.'' I didn't know if I wanted her to take me seriously or not. I thought I did, but it scared me.

''You'd hate it. You'll never give up sleeping in late, setting your own hours, working all night if you feel like it . . . you wouldn't even get up with me if I were here all the time. And I don't want to see you turn into a regimented little payroll grabber, I don't think I'd like you at all. You'd hate it, and after a while you'd hate me . . . we're not ready for anything more than we've got, are we, Paul?'' She looked at her watch again, still talking very fast, and said, ''I've got to get moving, I have to be at the bank in forty minutes.'' She gulped the coffee and dashed off to the bedroom, leaving me to think about it. She was right, of course, neither of us was a very good bet for something permanent. That's what we need to keep the divorce rate down, a little logic in these things. I wondered why I didn't feel better about it.

Steen came to the back door about noon. I'd never have recognized him, he looked like an out-of-work handyman trying for the job of polishing the furniture. For the benefit of anybody listening from the outside we went through the spiel before I let him in. ''Steen!'' I said. ''Hey, I'm glad to see you, where you been? You look awful.''

"Not so loud, Paul. Look, can I come in, I've got trouble."

"Well, sure, you've always been welcome . . . where you been?" I got the door closed behind us, glad to be through with that funny business. An actor I'm not. It probably sounded natural enough, and anyway there wasn't much chance that anybody'd heard it.

"Seen the papers, Paul?" he asked.

"Yeah. You're right there on page four. Rotten picture of you, somebody'd have to be looking at you to identify you from it."

"That's the idea, anyway. They'll probably come across something better before long. School annual has one that looks enough like me, better than what they've got. I'm clean, by the way. They made sure of that."

"Good. So the only people who'll know you're here will be the ones Janie tells about it. Lunch?"

He nodded, and I threw something together. I like to cook when there's somebody to appreciate it, and after lunch I started peeling vegetables and chopping things up for a teriyaki. There'd be the three of us for supper that night in a secure house. It might be our last like that.

After dinner, Janie and I went out to make the rounds so we'd be seen together. We wanted the connection firmly established, which was OK by me. Steen was in one of the little upstairs bedrooms with all the blinds down. Janie and I crawled through most of the taverns, got back to the house before midnight since she was still a working girl and we didn't usually go to parties except on weekends. As we came in Steen whispered an all right and closed his bedroom door. Somehow I never got around to taking her home that night either.

About noon the next day the doorbell rang. Steen scooted down to the basement and I went to answer it. Out on the porch was a guy, maybe forty-five, dressed in a dark suit with shiny spots at the elbows. He had steel-rimmed glasses and a McNamara haircut parted in the middle, a round face with a red-over-pink complexion. There was dandruff on his coat, but not as much as the horrible examples nobody speaks to on TV. "Mr. Paul Crane?" he asked.

"Yes. What can I do for you?"

"It is, I think, what I can do for you. I represent Information Associates, Mr. Crane. I doubt that you have ever heard of us. Can I come in and tell you about our services?" He was an apologetic talker, as if he were afraid I'd slam the door in his face. I wondered who'd slammed the last one.

As I let him in, I looked at him and felt a sour taste. OK, Shearing had called it right. No question, we were in contact with the free enterprise spies, for what good that could do, but I saw why Shearing didn't seem too confident that this particular operation was going to work. He'd better rely on his other ones, this man was a real loser.

"Come on in." I opened the big sliding doors directly into my living room office and showed him a chair over in the corner by the built-in glass-front bookcases. "Beer, coffee, what have you?" I asked.

"Why, I think a bottle of beer would be excellent," he said. He looked a little surprised when I got the glasses out of the lower part of the cooler and drew a pair. "Uh, yes, thank you."

I grinned to myself and made a bet that before the afternoon was over he'd find a reason to be alone in that room if it killed him. "Now, mister. . . ."

"Prufro. Dr. Arthur Prufro. With a 'u.' As I said, with Information Associates. We buy and sell information, Mr. Crane." He folded his hands across his lap and gave me a confidential look. "And I think it is safe to say that we have many advantages. Not only price-wise, but our transactions are always completely confidential. The sellers and buyers do not meet. No matter what information is being sold.''

"I see. Well, I'm sorry, Dr. Prufro, but I'm afraid I'm not in the market for information at the moment.''

"Oh, I didn't expect you to buy, sir. My associates and I have reason to believe you might have something to sell. Or to be more exact, that you have, uh, friends, who might have talents that are not, at present, marketable to the usual sources.'' He tossed off a good slug of beer which surprised me. He was such a dainty-acting character that I thought he'd be a sipper. "It's a very bad situation right now, Mr. Crane. There are many distinguished scientists in this country who are not, because of asinine regulations, allowed to do the work they have devoted their lives to. Are they then to starve? Live off charity? We at Information Associates don't see it that way. We think that scientific knowledge belongs to all mankind, but that the scientist who discovers it should be rewarded commensurate with his, uh, talents. I thought you might know someone in that situation.''

"Suppose I did. Just what would you do?''

"Why, we'd like to speak with him, Mr. Crane. Ascertain, as it were, the value of what he has to sell. Then we find a buyer for him.''

"And your commission?''

"It is flexible, but generally around fifty per cent. After all, we take the risks in arranging that buyer and seller, uh, do business without connecting them . . . it is only fair that we should take half the income. And of course we pay all expenses out of our half.''

"Yeah.'' I looked at him without much enthusiasm. If this was a sample of the people who were going to lead us to the Chinese Intelligence Service, USA (West Coast) Branch, we were leaning on a pretty weak reed. "Suppose for a moment''—hell, I was catching his formal speech disease myself. "Let's just suppose I've got a buddy who might be able to do business with you, but he'd be a little embarrassed to be seen in public. He might want to keep his location confidential, let's say. How might we get together?"

Prufro nodded. "Now we come down to business, don't we? We don't have to meet Dr. Hoorne at your house, Mr. Crane, although it would be a lot easier on both of us if you would simply bring him out to meet me now."

"Who said anything about. . . ."

"You don't have to," he interrupted smoothly. "We know perfectly well that Dr. Steen Hoorne, wanted by the FBI for questioning in connection with security violations, is in this house. He was here last night and has not left by any exit, so there's no argument. We'd like to talk to him." He drained the beer. "Excellent. May I have some more?"

"Sure." I tossed off mine and poured again for both of us. "I don't know what you're talking about, you understand."

"I didn't expect you to admit it. All we want to do is meet Dr. Hoorne and make him an offer. Surely there's nothing to be frightened of about that."

"If you're who you say you are. Look, I don't know anything about Steen, but he is an old friend of mine. Suppose I could reach him, just how would we know you aren't working for the FBI? There doesn't seem to be any way to prove your good intentions, Dr. Prufro."

He sighed, shook his head sadly, every gesture exaggerated for effect. "We know more about you than you think, Mr. Crane. For example. For the past two nights you have had an overnight visitor, Miss Janie Youngs, a bank officer whose employer would be quite shocked to discover her nocturnal habits. . . . Calm down, sir, I am merely giving you a demonstration. Also, since noon yesterday Dr. Steen Hoorne has been a guest in this house, and he has been very careful about being observed from the outside. I could give you the exact times you and Miss Youngs have entered and left this house if you'd care to have them.''

''I know when I came in and out. Look here. . . .''

''No, sir. You look, Mr. Crane. You really have no choice. If I am in fact an official representative of the government, you are doomed. I have already proved to you that I have had this house watched. I could have your guest arrested immediately if that were my purpose. Why don't you simply accept me for what I say I am? I am determined to talk to Dr. Hoorne, and there is no point in waiting. You will notice, by the way, that we have said nothing to the bank about Miss Youngs . . .''

''You better not either.'' I stood over him with my fists clenched. ''I'll take you into small pieces.''

''Ah, gallantry.'' I wanted to push the mocking tone back down his throat even while I stood there waiting for him to swallow the hook. ''You have nothing to fear from us, sir, as long as you cooperate; and you stand to make a great deal of money. Come now, we mean neither you nor Dr. Hoorne any mischief. He's no use to us in jail.''

I gave a long sigh, sat for a moment as if I was thinking it over. ''Just a second.'' I went out to the hall and called down the stairs. ''Come on up, partner, you've got a visitor.''

While Steen was climbing out of the basement, I slipped around to the kitchen and looked through the crack in the door. I could just see the corner of the room Dr. Prufro was sitting in. He was leaning over, doing something to the bottom shelf of the low bookcase under the window. I waited until he had sat back up, leaned back as if he had never moved, before I led Steen into the office. As I did I made sure that Dr. Prufro saw the Luger under my belt.

"There is no need for firearms," he said nervously. "No need at all. Ah, Dr. Hoorne? I am Dr. Arthur Prufro. Perhaps you have heard of me?"

"No." Steen looked at him closely. "No," he said again. He hunched his shoulders, looked around apprehensively as if he expected armed men to come out of the walls. "Who are you, and what do you want?"

"Why, I've come to do you a favor, Dr. Hoorne. It seems to my associates and me that you have earned considerable more money for your research than you have actually been paid. We have clients who will pay well for, uh, for research that you have already done. Not to mention an offer of further employment in your field if you like."

"The hell with employment. What I know is worth about a million dollars. Are you in a position to pay that much?" Steen glanced around, grabbed a bottle of Scotch off the shelf and poured himself a healthy slug. "That's the offer. You interested? If not, I think Paul can find somebody who'll pay it."

Prufro hesitated, a little surprised. "Well. Your directness is refreshing after your friend's circumlocutions. You realize, of course, that before they would pay that much my clients must be convinced that you have information worth that money? I'm not trying to lower the price, Dr. Hoorne, after all we stand to gain as much as you by keeping the price up. But perhaps you will not be able to get quite so much. Perhaps, instead of a million, only half that. . . . That would be a lot of money for a man who at the moment does not even dare go down the street for a cup of coffee." He slicked his hair carefully on each side of his head, although it didn't need brushing. "You are, uh, willing to negotiate on the price? And to offer the proofs that our clients will require?"

"Something might be arranged. Paul knows more about this kind of thing than I do. I never had anything to do with business, I just make lasers play games. What proofs do you want?"

"Well. We must convince them that you are making an offer in good faith . . . that you have something to sell and are in fact willing to sell it. There should be several ways to accomplish that." The talk about a million bucks had got to him. I noticed that his shoes were breaking down a little, and his handkerchief was clean but had spots on it as if it had been sent to the laundry a little too often. His suit wasn't new, either. Dr. Prufro wasn't starving but he wasn't rolling in money and his share of a big score was going to his head. It might have gone to mine but I knew I couldn't keep the money.

"Paul," Steen said carefully. "We could travel a long way on even a quarter million, you and I. We could be big men in South America."

"Yeah." I looked thoughtful for a second. "OK, Dr. Prufro, somebody's got to take a chance. It might as well be me, I haven't got a smell of that kind of dough any other way." I fished around in my pocket, got out keys and opened a little strongbox under the drafting table. "Here. This ought to be worth something. Nobody knows it's missing, the certificate of destruction was made out properly, never mind how. Nobody'll ever be looking for this. By the way, once you walk out of here it can't be traced to me either. I'm willing to let you take it on speculation. You see what you can get for it and bring me my share. That ought to prove that you've got a source with something worth selling. . . ."

"Yes." Prufro examined it with interest. "This seems quite authentic, Mr. Crane. Missile base emplacements . . . yes, not exactly scientific information, but certainly valuable. And it does, as you suggest, demonstrate a willingness to sell."

"I've got more along the same lines," I told him. He looked eager. "Let's see what you get for that first. How much would you say?''

"Perhaps ten thousand dollars, five thousand for you.'' Prufro was hanging onto the document as if he thought I'd snatch it away.

He'd passed the first test. He wasn't trying to shortchange us, the opposite in fact, he'd never get that much for it. It remained to see if he could get anything at all, and if so, whether we'd see any of it. I tried to look nervous. "Just keep in mind, Dr. Prufro, I've got more like that for sale, and Steen has something even more valuable in his head. Keep that image of a one and six zeroes firmly in sight at all times. Concentrate on that if you ever get the idea of pocketing my share of what you've got in your hands.''

He stood, shook his head sadly. "So much distrust, Mr. Crane. A real pity. But we hope to prove to you that we act in good faith. Let's shake hands like gentlemen, shall we?'' I took his hand, a flabby cold thing with no grip. Prufro shook with Steen, then excused himself. I watched him plod apologetically off the stoop, then nodded at Hoorne.

"What do you think?'' Steen asked me.

"Damned if I know. Can't be cops, you'd be in the jug right now. How in hell did they know you were here? Those guys must have a pretty good organization, you know that?''

"Do you believe that guff about them being brokers? I think they're commies. The creep looked like a commie,'' Steen snorted and clinked the Scotch bottle against the glass, not pouring anything.

"Better not drink so much,'' I told him. "And get over that attitude. So they're commies. You just keep in mind, they're the guys who are going to pay us for the contents of your head, my friend. Let's face it, it would take us time to find a buyer. We can't advertise.'' I lit my pipe, flopped in the big leather chair. "Here, put a record on and let's relax.''

Beethoven's *Fifth* boomed out of the stereo again, and I got the box Dykeman had left, fitted the earphones to it and jammed them into my ears so I couldn't hear the music. Then I tuned across the dial, turning the knob very slowly. About halfway over, there was the *Fifth*, loud and clear. I nodded to Steen.

"Uh, Paul?" he said softly.

"Yeah?"

"Oh, nothing." He walked slowly around the room, fiddling with his pipe. "Do you think this is going to work out all right? I'm a bit scared. What if they—what if they don't pay us?"

"They'll pay us. The main thing is to keep them from knowing we're worried." I waved him out toward the dining room. "I mean, we've got the edge. You really do know everything about those tame ruby lights of yours."

He walked along, giving me a solo act about how nervous he was, with me telling him not to worry, we'd make sure they didn't cheat us. By the time he got to the far edge of the dining room I couldn't really understand him over the music. I let the record run out and tested again with him walking around some more. It turned out that you could hear anything in the living room office, record or not, and could make out most of what was being said in the other rooms although with a record on it was a little garbled. Steen and I went into the kitchen to start on the dinner. We didn't go near the low bookshelf in the office.

5

DINNER WAS A little strained. Even though my tests showed their bug probably wouldn't pick up conversations out in the kitchen, it seemed safer to play it straight all the time. That put Steen in the role of a scared man with a million bucks' worth of military secrets who drank too much, me as the guy who'd stumbled into something good and wasn't letting go, and Janie as my girl friend. Her role was the toughest of all. She was supposed to know all about us, but not that we knew she was feeding Prufro's people information. From their point of view she was attaching herself to me as their inside girl, ready to report on any changes in our attitude. From ours, she didn't know about the racket, she was just my mistress.

It made it hard for her to play, and she fell back on a kind of strumpet act, a girl determined to make me think she was fascinated with me. I didn't like her that way. I mean, I was perfectly happy to have her go nuts about me, but not to act like it for the benefit of the damned electron box in the bookcase. Besides, it got me confused as to what was the real Janie and which act was what. She couldn't come out of the role even in the bedroom. Not that I blamed her, changing acts all the time is tough, but I'd like to have had the real girl back.

If, I kept trying not to think, there was a real girl under there somewhere. I mean, who was she? Not Miss Youngs, loan counselor and officer at a local bank. Not the medium-grade strumpet hanging on to me for the money I might pick up selling out my country. An Agency girl on an assignment? In which case, what was the assignment, and how did I fit into her orders, and when the box wasn't there was it still an act, this time for me courtesy of Shearing and Company? As I said, I tried to avoid thoughts like that, but they kept coming around, and in that place there wasn't any way to get the problem out in the open.

We went through the night and the next day playing games. The day after, about the same time as before, Prufro showed up on the stoop.

"I have good news for you," he said after he got inside.

"Fine." I showed him into the office. Since I hadn't opened the drapes from the night before it seemed safe enough to bring Steen in.

"Yes. Excellent news." He opened a little attaché case. "Not, perhaps, quite as much as I thought at first, but still a healthy sum. Three thousand dollars."

It made quite a package. I handed some of it to Steen and began counting my pile, while Prufro sat back with a little smile, watching us while he drank my beer and made like Father Christmas. "It seems to be all here," we told him.

"Of course. Now, I believe you mentioned some other documents?" He didn't rub his hands together, but he might as well have. He had on a new pair of shoes, the soles hardly had a scratch.

I looked at him thoughtfully. "Yeah. Well, I can risk a couple more. When do we get to the big show?"

"Ah. For that we must have samples. Dr. Hoorne, would you be willing to meet with a member of Information Associates and discuss your specialty? Give him, shall we say, something to use to convince our clients of your value?"

"What about it, Paul?" Steen asked. He gave Prufro a searching look, then turned back to me. "Should we?"

"Why not? We've come this far. What do you make of those documents, Dr. Prufro?"

He had been thumbing through them, shook his head sadly. "I regret to say that the two of them together are probably worth no more than, oh, ten thousand dollars. Perhaps not that much. Our buyers have informed us that missile base information is not really their highest priority. I gather that they have, uh, other sources. Free enterprise has the disadvantage of competition, you know," he added pompously.

"Yeah. When?"

"Oh, we could pay you quite soon. This evening, perhaps. Under the circumstances we would be prepared to advance you four thousand dollars. If we sell them for more than eight we will give you the balance due. Is that satisfactory?" I nodded. He turned to Steen. "Have you reached a decision, Dr. Hoorne?"

"Paul says it's all right. What do you want to know?"

Prufro shook his head, a precise little gesture. "Regretfully, that is not my specialty. And unfortunately, the man you must meet does not care to come to this house. You will have to meet him."

"I'll be damned," Steen said vigorously.

"So much distrust," Prufro observed. "Very sad.

What could happen to you anywhere else that cannot be arranged here? And you must not think you are the only ones taking risks. No, if it were left to me we would conclude our business here, but my associate insists that you come to meet him. It will be quite safe." He touched his fingers together, clutching the documents against his belly with his wrists. "Surely we can manage something? This has been very profitable, we mustn't spoil it."

"What the hell, Steen, he's right. If they're going to turn you in to the cops, they can do it from here."

"Yeah." He poured another slug of Scotch, tossed it off. That drinking act was great for short spurts, but I wished he'd thought of something else. He was going to pickle himself if we ever had a long conference with these jokers. "All right."

Prufro gave us a big oily smile. "Mr. Crane, be at the laundromat behind the Pay and Save drug store at precisely eight this evening and answer the telephone. You will be told where to meet us. Be ready to leave at once, and make no calls after you have talked to us." He stood, gave us another smile. "In this business it is sometimes desirable to be a bit melodramatic."

I agreed, but I didn't think he'd appreciate my observations on the subject.

I was in the laundromat at the right time, and the phone rang as advertised. It was Prufro on the other end, of course, and he told me to go out to the Red Dog Tavern in Carnation. Somebody would let us know what to do after that.

It seemed a hell of a long way to drive. Carnation is a little hick dairy town northeast of Seattle in the middle of some farming country and wooded hills with trout streams. I knew about it, I'd had clients— back when I had clients—who had me put in access roads and bridges not far from there. A few miles

east of Carnation there's a complex of woodlands
and beaver dams with some of the best fishing near
Seattle. I just hope nobody finds out about them so
the water isn't churning with lures on opening day
the way most streams are now.

Carnation was a long way off, but it had the advantage that nobody was likely to recognize Steen. I
made no objections; I mean, we weren't really being
hard to get, we just wanted the other side to think we
were.

The drive out in my Barracuda was dull. We took
that car because it was still trying to rain and the
leaky top on the TR was just too discouraging. The
Red Dog turned out to be a big barn of a place with
sawdust on the floor and thick wood tables. It was
half empty, the other half full of farmers tossing off
a few after a hard day's milking or whatever they do
around there. For laughs they had TV in one corner
and a couple of fights in the other. When one of the
fights would get out of hand, the bartender, a big
character about six five and weighing easily three
hundred, would come around the counter, motion
to a skinny guy who sat at one end, and between
them they'd shift the whole fight out in the street. I
watched it the first time and didn't believe it, but it
happened again, four guys pounding away in a free-
for-all, and here comes this human moose with his
beanpole assistant moving in on them. They sort of
surrounded them with their arms and out went the
fight, a living entity not just a collection of people.

Steen nodded. "I have seen that before, in Ballard
when I was young. Not many bartenders know how
to do that, now."

"I'll bet they don't. Looks like a handy trick. . . ."

The phone rang. The bartender shouted "Crane?"
and I went to take it. It didn't take long. I said
"Crane" and the phone answered "Paradise Lodge.
Four miles south of you there's a turnoff. A mile east

on that is the lodge. Of course you will telephone no one.''

We got in the car before I told Steen. I didn't have to telephone anyone, my car was wired. At least it was supposed to be, and somebody should have been close enough to hear what went on in it, but we'd seen no signs of company. If the company was going to be any use, we wouldn't.

The Paradise Lodge was a rundown old motel built back when this road must have got considerably more traffic than it did now. Paint was peeling off the white clapboard cabins, and the only one with a light in it was number four. On the way we'd picked up an escort, someone driving about a hundred yards behind us, obviously matching his speed to us. When we pulled up at cabin four a new Chevy parked just far enough away so I couldn't see the plates and a girl got out.

She was quite a dish, about medium-size with a healthy pink face and long carefully brushed hair. She had on a pair of those fancy new slacks, the thin ones with flowers and things all over them. There was a blouse made out of the same kind of cloth, thin cotton, but a different pattern. The outfit included about five scarves. There was one over her head, another around her waist, and a couple more artistically knotted together around her neck. An unbuttoned white leather coat completed the outfit. She grinned at us, a young clean-cut-girl grin. "Go on in," she invited.

There was just one guy in there, a young fellow no more than twenty-five. He looked at the girl possessively for a second, then noticed us. "Any problem, Bev?"

"No. They came right out of the tavern and drove straight here. There wasn't any more traffic on the road." She took off the coat and threw it across the bed. "Something to drink? We don't have a big variety, but there's Scotch. You like beer, don't you, Mr. Crane?''

"Yes, thanks. Steen, you better stick to beer after all the Scotch."

"I don't need a nursemaid," he said irritably. "Yeah, give me beer. Thanks."

"OK, who are you?" I demanded. The two of them were just kids. The boy was an average-looking boy, clean-shaven, close-cut brown hair, freckles, a personnel man's image of the perfect junior executive. His sports shirt was clean and well pressed, a subdued pastel green, and his slacks were some kind of wool, well tailored. I don't know what I'd expected, but he wasn't it. He was wearing something, a political pin or button, and I leaned over to take a closer look. It showed a chain with a broken link, and in small letters the broken link was labeled "laissez-faire." I looked puzzled, then saw that the girl was wearing one too.

"I'm Dick," he said. "I know something about lasers, and you know who I represent. Let's get on with it, shall we?" He was working at being serious and businesslike, not saying anything unnecessary.

"Sure," Steen answered. "It's been a long drive. So you know lasers, tell me what you think of Mayer's work with gaseous plasmas." At least that's what I think he said. It might have been something else. I'm just a civil engineer and when I took physics there weren't any lasers in my books. The kid made some kind of appropriate response, Steen looked surprised, and I wandered over to the corner where the girl was sitting. There wasn't any point in my listening to them.

"Mind telling me what the pins are for?" I asked her.

"Just what they say. Support of free enterprise," she told me. She opened her bag to show me some others. "Legalize abortion," "Legalize marijuana,"

"God grows his own" were some of them. "We believe in freedom," she said.

"That's why you're collecting information to sell to the commies?"

She looked disappointed. "You're selling it, you know."

"For money, doll. I don't brag about it. If I could make a good living some other way, I'd probably try it."

"Yes, but you see, that's what's wrong with everything. No freedom. Your friend there is not free to sell his ideas to the highest bidder. The government makes him a slave. They did that to Dick, too. Tried to keep him in the army, pay him a lieutenant's wages to work on projects worth millions."

"If the Russians win this thing, there won't be much freedom," I protested. It wasn't much of an argument, and the last thing I needed to do was talk the kids out of whatever idiocy they'd got into, but it was an interesting point of view.

She smiled again, a superior sort of smile. I recognized it immediately. All the little leftists from my ex-wife's old crowd had it. Pity for the poor dope who was just so ignorant he couldn't see the truth.

Except for the expression she had a nice face. The thin slacks and blouse didn't leave much doubt that the rest of her was constructed pretty well. I'd had worse people to endure for an evening. "If we had real freedom, the communists would never have a chance," she said seriously. "Slavery can't compete with freedom, but it has to be real freedom, not this drifting to slavery we've got now."

She had a lot more, about the military, and government contracts, and taxes, and government monopolies in education, a ready-made spiel she'd given so often I doubt she even knew what she was saying anymore. A lot of it made sense, but everything was carried out to its logical conclusion. I don't know

much about politics, but I do know that nobody can
live where everything has to be logical. People aren't
very logical, and I think I'm glad of it.

"Dr. Prufro one of your true believers?" I asked
her.

"I guess so. He's very effective. Quite a good
scientist." I got the impression that Prufro knew
something about nuclei. He seemed to have made
most of his discoveries in government laboratories
and resented hell out of the fact that he couldn't sell
his talents on the open market.

Steen and the boy talked for an hour. After a little
while Dick got out a clipboard and wrote furiously. I
gathered he was getting what he wanted. Finally they
finished and had a last drink. Dick nodded, gave us a
half smile. "You do know the subject, Dr. Hoorne.
We won't have any trouble selling your information.
There's just one problem—can you get to Los
Angles?"

"Los Angeles? For God's sake, who'd go there?"
Steen demanded.

"Our buyers. They're very cautious. They will
want to talk to you themselves. I'm sure you know
you haven't given us anything worth the kind of
money you ask. Since their expert won't come up
here, we'll have to go to him."

"L.A." Hoorne turned to me. "Can we get
there?"

While I was supposedly thinking about that, Dick
reached under the bed, took out a paper sack. "This
is yours, it may help your decision." I shook out a
pile of money, twenties and tens mostly. "There's
four thousand as agreed," Dick told us. "We've
been honest with you. And a trip out of the rain will
do you good. Help that cough, Dr. Hoorne."

Steen had coughed a couple of times, but I hadn't
paid any attention. He wasn't sick. "When do you
want us there?" I asked.

"May fourth. A little less than three weeks. You'll take Miss Youngs, of course?"

"What the hell has she got to do with this?"

"Nothing. It seemed to me as good a way to make contact as any. Have her register in the Hollywood Roosevelt Hotel and we'll get a message to her. That way you won't be asked to trust us." He didn't add that it was unlikely that we would, but he thought it.

"When we get there we'll want to see some money before anything else happens," I warned them. "Real money, not little stuff like this."

"I don't call four thousand dollars tax-free little stuff," he told us. "But you're right, we'll show you some money. We're very businesslike, Mr. Crane, it isn't our fault that we have to go through these mysterious ceremonies to meet. We've a right to do what we're doing, but the government doesn't agree. We'll keep our part of the agreement."

"Maybe," I grunted. "OK. Janie registers at the Hollywood Roosevelt and you'll let her know how to find you. She's not in on any of this, you know. Be careful what you say to her."

Dick was good, he didn't react at all, but behind me I could hear Bev give a little snort, choking back a laugh. I didn't look around because I didn't want them to know I'd caught it. Dick covered for her nicely. "Surely she knows that Dr. Hoorne is wanted by the FBI and that he is in your house. If she doesn't know he's wanted, she's the only person in Seattle."

"Yeah," I growled. "I forgot you had my house watched. OK, she knows he's wanted and she doesn't give a damn. He's my friend and she's on my side. I'd still rather she didn't find out about treason. It might upset her."

"We'll spare her feelings," Dick said smoothly. "Well, that's about it. You go east and we'll go west. We'll wait until you've driven away if you don't mind."

I nodded. If the boys outside hadn't got a look at
the car by now—nuts, I thought. They knew about
this before I did. I kept forgetting exactly where
Janie fit into all this.

6

WE LEFT THEM standing by cabin four and drove east on the road. The country around there was flat, nothing but a few farmhouses a mile or so apart, the road a two-lane asphalt ribbon lined with tall trees. I wasn't sure of the way, having looked at the map only to find the route we'd taken from Seattle. I remembered that east of Carnation the road joined up with another highway to the ski areas in the pass, but I wasn't too familiar with it. It didn't seem to matter, we'd find a gas station somewhere and ask directions. For that matter we could turn around and go back, although I hated to do that.

The road started to climb up the side of a bluff, and I knew we'd missed a turn somewhere. We were headed up into the logging country where the trout streams were. I thought I might even remember the road, and if I was right it wouldn't take us back to Seattle.

"About time to look for another route," I told Steen.

"There's a car behind us," he said slowly.

"I expect there is. Probably Shearing's troops wondering where in hell we're leading them. I think

57

we're lost, boys,'' I added loudly.

"Yeah,'' He lit his pipe and I wished I weren't driving so I could fill mine. "They're catching up to us,'' he observed.

I could see that in the rear-view mirror, and slowed down to make it easier. The car came up fast, a big Detroit job. It got bumper to bumper with us, honked a couple of times although there was plenty of room to pass.

"If he does and it's Shearing's people, he knows the signal,'' I pulled over to the right to let them get by, and the car came up nearly alongside. The window rolled down, and somebody pointed a gun at us.

"Stop!'' he commanded. At least that's what I think he was saying. I wasn't staying around to find out. I dropped into second gear and slammed the accelerator to the floorboards as soon as I saw the gun, even before he had it really pointed at us. The big four-barrel carburetors cut in and we shot out ahead before they could react. Then I was covered with flying chunks of glass.

"Jesus Christ, he shot at us!'' Steen shouted. "The rear window's out.''

It sure was. That window makes up about half the aft surface area of the car, one of the biggest windows ever put in an automobile, and it's bent in a series of compound curves that must have a hell of a lot of internal stress because it hadn't just starred, the whole thing disintegrated into half-inch chunks of tinted glass. They were all over, in my hair, strung out across the dash, everywhere.

I poured on the steam, letting the car reach her limits of skid on the twisting road. For a wonder the rain had stopped while we were in the motel but the road was still wet. We skidded around a corner, took a left-hand branch of a fork far too fast and I had to brake like hell for the blind corner just beyond it, dropping to second and taking her up to the redline on the tach coming out.

"They're falling back a little," Steen shouted.

"They ought to. You recognize anybody?"

"No. Two men. I didn't get much of a look at them, I was watching the gun, but I don't think I've seen either of them before."

We had a relatively long straight stretch, and I went through the gears to fourth, reaching for top speed, but the car behind had more power than we did. It was catching up fast, and I prayed for more curves. When it drew up behind us I saw orange flashes in the mirror. A reaction was trying to set in, but if I ever gave way to it I'd be too scared to drive. My hands on the wheel and shift knob were white, and I eased off on the grip. On the third flash something whizzed past my ear and took out the front windshield. A chunk of glass blew back, slashing my cheek.

"Here," I told Steen. "Shoot back." I handed him the Luger I'd been packing around in my belt all evening. I hadn't even remembered it until then.

I was glad to see he knew how to cock the piece, it meant he might have fired one before. He turned, braced himself against the seat, and fired three shots, slowly, aiming each one out the back where the rear window had been. The car behind us dropped back a few yards and he held his fire.

"You hit anything?" I asked.

"Possibly. There was a time when I wasn't too bad with one of these."

"Good. How well do you drive?"

"Not well at all."

"Better." We had the right people in the right jobs. "My driving's a hell of a lot better than my shooting."

The road seemed to lead us nowhere, curving back

in the general direction of Carnation but there weren't any lights anymore. We ought to be getting out of the hills pretty soon at the speed we were going, but I saw no signs of it.

"Hold on, here they come again," Steen shouted. "Yahoooo!"

"Jesus Christ, an enthusiast," I started to say. I don't think I finished the comment. The big car got up closer and the orange flashes started again, the Luger went off with another string of three, and I lost control of the car. We skidded across the road, I caught her, overcorrected, and we went across to the other side, fishtailing down the blacktop, just at the edge of losing it, slowing down rapidly. "Save the bloody ammunition!" I shouted. "They hit a tire!"

"They've stopped," Steen said. He was quite calm. "I think they crashed. There's another car coming up, it's stopped too." By that time I had control and we rolled to a halt, the blown-out rear tire thumping along. I pulled over to the side of the road and began to shake.

There were more shots from behind us. It sounded like a regimental battle for a second, then it was quiet. A couple of crickets went back to their sere-nade, and somewhere way off an owl screamed.

I pulled myself together. "Out of here!" I said. "Come on, man, into the woods!" Somehow I got hold of the money, although I don't know what I thought I'd do with it.

"Yeah." We jumped out, dashed across the road and into the trees. Steen thundered along like a buf-falo.

"Keep quiet, you dolt," I growled. We stopped to listen.

"Crane?" someone called. "Crane? This is George. Your escort, damn it. Get your ass out here."

Steen looked at me. I nodded. "I know him. One

of Shearing's local talent. Let's go see what he wants.''

The last time I'd seen George, he was a skinny little runt with buck teeth and glasses and I thought he was ugly. His appearance hadn't changed a bit, but he looked damn good to me now. He was standing by the wrecked car, which I saw was one of the larger Pontiacs. The windshield was out, a bullet had plowed a long furrow across the hood, and there were a lot of neat holes punched in one side. Two big guys in dark suits were stretched out beside it, and they weren't moving.

"Know them?" George asked.

I shook my head and Steen said, "No." We looked at them carefully to make sure, and I started shaking again.

"Pull yourself together, man," George muttered. "Get him a drink, Stevens. I've got something in the glove compartment." He took me by the shoulders, digging his fingers into my collarbone. They were strong fingers for a little guy. "Come on, Crane, you did fine. You guys moved out of there so fast I thought we'd never catch you. Who did the shooting?"

I pointed to Hoorne.

"Good work. You took the driver out. One right in the chest. Don't know how he stopped the car before he died. Only left us the other one." He took the bottle his partner was holding out, opened it and handed it to me. "Have a big slug, you won't be driving home."

I got the liquor down, not noticing what it was. It burned my throat, but it felt good, and my legs decided to hold still. "Thanks. Thanks for being back there, too."

"We weren't needed. Told you, you killed the driver. One shot. All that's left for us is the cleanup, which could be a bit sticky if somebody runs across

us here. Good thing there's no traffic. Come on, get
in the car, Stevens can stand watch until I send reinforcements.''

"You can't radio for them?"

He laughed. "No. This little short-range bug to
your car is pretty secure, but we don't go in for radio
calls much. Come on, we've got to get to a phone and
report.''

I let myself be loaded into the front seat of
George's Buick, while Steen climbed in back. "You
going to keep that bottle all night?" Hoorne asked. I
took another slug and passed it back.

"Want to tell me about it?" George asked. I nodded and got it out, found it was easier after I got
started. Hell, these were tough friends, I didn't want
to look like a coward. I started to apologize about the
shakes, but George cut me off. "You came through
all right when you were needed. Everybody gets a little shook when it's over. So they made one try at
stopping you, then bang! huh? Not too serious a try
to stop you either, like they were supposed to make
the attempt but weren't really very enthusiastic about
it. Those guys were mainly out to kill you, you got
any theories why?''

"Nothing but the obvious ones . . . but there aren't
any obvious ones, are there? Dead, Steen's no more
use to them. Could it be the money?" I showed him
the bag I was still holding on to.

"How would anybody know you had it? The information people sure wouldn't give you three grand,
then try to kill you for four.''

"For that matter," Steen asked, "how did they
know we would be there? It had to be someone from
the Information Associates group, no one else knew
we would be out here tonight. Remember the
elaborate precautions they took to keep it a secret.''

"Yeah." George looked thoughtful. "Well, here's
a gas station. Excuse me while I use the phone.

Crane, you better stand by, the chief might want to talk to you."

"Sure." I got my pipe out, began filling it, remembering how I'd almost slowed down to do it before and wondering if they'd have caught us if I had. George was gone a long time, came back with a puzzled look. "You better go talk to him, Paul, there's something funny happening tonight."

"You're telling me?" I went to the phone booth. "Crane."

"On the telephone, you're Larry. You never remember, do you?"

"Yeah. All right, sir, Larry reporting." There wasn't much question about it being Shearing. He's the only guy I know who sounds the same over the telephone, over a radio, or in the room with you. There's a flat electronic quality to his voice that I've never quite figured out.

"Report on your meeting," he said. I did, describing the two kids and how we were supposed to meet them in Los Angeles.

"Excellent. You'd have had problems staying in Seattle anyway, the Bureau's looking for you."

"What?"

"Someone gave the Bureau a tip that Hoorne was staying with you, and a couple of their agents went out to your house with a search warrant an hour ago. They almost got Janie, but she was lucky, she saw them when they went in. They're waiting there for you now. Add that to the two gentlemen in the Pontiac, and it looks very much as if someone doesn't like you."

I thought about that one for a minute. "Any idea who?"

"None. The Bureau's tip was anonymous, as I understand it. I could be wrong, but I don't think so. The two gunmen tonight are hired talent. I doubt they made any serious attempt to take you alive."

"They didn't."

"So George says. I haven't made any sense out of this yet." He was quiet for a while, then asked, "Is there anything in your house to connect you with Dr. Hoorne?"

I thought that one over. The only thing Steen had brought with him was his clothes, and he was wearing them. "Nothing but fingerprints. If they think to take those, they'll know."

Shearing chuckled. "No they won't. The prints they have on file are not Dr. Hoorne's. Excellent. Then they won't be looking for you that hard. They might put out a bulletin on you, but you won't get your picture in the papers or anything like that if we can keep the local police from connecting you with the shooting tonight. Of course, your cars are out as means of transportation."

"The TR's out. The Barracuda's in pretty bad shape anyway."

"We'll get it fixed for you. We'll cover your tracks in the shooting too. The thing now is to arrange transportation for you to Los Angeles."

"I can arrange my own," I growled. "I'm not sure who's tipped who about what, Mr. Shearing, but the only two outfits who knew where I was going tonight were Information Associates and your crowd. It doesn't make sense that one of your people put the finger on us, but it makes as much as saying that the information boys wanted to kill their meal ticket. I'd rather do without your transportation if you don't mind."

"How do you expect to get over a thousand miles with every road watched? You can't just go to an airport or bus station, you know. They're serious about trying to find Dr. Hoorne."

"I know. Don't worry, I've got a way."

"You will tell me what you intend to do. This is ridiculous, I can't take a chance on some hick cop picking you up hitchhiking." He thought for a second. "You fly, don't you? Have you got some crazy idea of renting an airplane and flying down?"

"I'm not going to hitchhike, and I wouldn't trust the airports either. Look, I'll tell you if you tell no one else. Nobody, not a soul, not a person in your agency. Deal?"

"Yes. You have a point, we don't really know where the leak is. Not that I agree it might be in my group, but if you have a good means of transportation, let's hear it."

"Good. You just have Janie available at the Hollywood Roosevelt. I'm going to sail us down."

"Sail? In that tiny little boat of yours? You're out of your mind."

"That's your reaction, uh? Good. Then if anybody thinks to look for my boat, which I doubt, they won't look far enough south. Most people think it's impossible to sail that far, sailboats just aren't thought of as a means of transportation. The Bureau will never think of it. I'll have George drop me off a couple of miles from the yacht basin and we'll walk. You'll have to arrange for one of the neighbors to feed my cat while we're gone, there's nothing else to worry about at the house. Let's see, the boat's got a good supply of stores on board and I've got plenty of money, we can buy provisions and outfits on the way."

"Isn't this a little silly? I can arrange transportation for you without going to all that trouble."

"It's the arranging that's the problem, Mr. Shearing. Just who in hell do you trust, and of those, who can *I* trust? Besides, we have to keep out of sight for a couple of weeks anyway. I can't think of a better way to do it."

Sitting in Neah Bay, I could think of a hell of a lot better ways to stay out of sight. We'd used up five days getting there, and we were running short of

time. Out there was a Pacific storm, nothing really
bad, but not something you want to go out in. I
thought of the alternative of calling Shearing and
having somebody come get us, but there was a problem with that: besides Shearing's man, who else
might show up? Remembering that Pontiac pulling
up behind us, and the glass spattering all over me,
there wasn't much choice in the matter. I went below
to check the storm sails.

7

THE WIND WAS blowing about twenty knots from the northwest and the sun was bright when we put out. Steen had got his hot shower, and I'd run my clothes through the dryer, but there hadn't been time for me to be sybaritic with the hot water. A shot of rum chased down by beer gave me the illusion of being warm, but that wouldn't last. Despite the sun, the wind was cold.

I was a little worried when we went past the Coast Guard station. They might send somebody to remind us about the storm. Because of that possibility, I lost a half hour sailing back down the Straits to give them the idea that we were running for Seattle and home base before we turned and beat back straight into the wind, using the motor to help us point higher. The sun was almost down when we sighted Tattoosh Island, a little granite bubble about a mile off Cape Flattery's wooded hills, looking alone and defenseless in the yellow twilight. The Coast Guard light there looked inviting and safe on its rocky base above the water, but surf was already pounding against the base of Tattoosh, throwing spray a hundred feet into the air. The Coast Guardsmen would get wet going from their white wooden barracks to the light spire.

In that weather we didn't dare use the little channel between Tattoosh and Flattery, but I wouldn't have anyway. What I wanted was sea room and lots of it. With a boat the size of *Witch* there's little chance that the wind and sea alone can do anything to her if you know what you're doing. The real danger is being run onto something hard, like land, mud, rocks, and the shore in general, and there was plenty of that around the lonely coast. We could be forced ashore by wind and sea, driven against rocks to leeward. Fire, fog, and a lee shore were the ancient fears of the old sea dogs, and things haven't changed much for the modern sailboat skipper.

We were ten miles off shore before dark, running almost broadside to the wind which had risen to thirty knots and was getting colder. *Witch* swooped along, enjoying herself, the waves lifting her high in the air, holding her there for an instant, then letting her slide sidewise into the troughs. There were high waves with big foaming whitecaps, but no breakers. It's only in places like Juan de Fuca that you get real breakers in less than a gale.

There was no chance of a hot dinner. Neither Steen nor I was up to making the stove work in that violent motion. I couldn't keep the pot on the stove without holding it, and I needed both hands to keep from being thrown in the cook fire. Steen didn't dare even go below. The change from the short chop of the straits to the long pendular up and down, up and down, of the Pacific was turning him slightly green. He huddled miserably in a corner of the cockpit.

"Take the helm," I told him.

"Uh, yes, but I'm, well, I'm not really up to it . . ."

"You'll feel better with something to do. Watch the horizon, just glance at the compass enough to keep us on course. Southwest as long as we can hold it." I waited for him to sit beside me on the stern seat, let him get the feel of the tiller before I let go. *Witch* was really lively, with the seas trying to throw her off it was difficult to hold a course. She had a weather helm that nearly tore your arm off. The wind was picking up, with each gust it didn't die back but blew harder, and I kept an eye out to windward. I didn't like the dark clouds out there at all. Overhead the sky was clear, a few stars visible in the last twilight, but to windward everything was ink black, no sign of sunset at all, giving an unshakable feeling of doom rushing down on us.

"Time to shorten sail," I told him. "I'm going to get the storm staysail up while there's still a little light." Actually I had cut that pretty fine, but I wanted to carry all the sail we could to get enough sea room to run away from the storm.

Going up on the foredeck was no picnic. I struggled into all my gear, waterproof trousers and jacket, sou'wester, sea boots, and put a horsecollar life jacket on over the whole mess. Not that it would do me any good; if I went overboard the chances of Steen being able to maneuver the boat in the rising seas after dark were just about nil. I passed a line around my waist, tied a bowline and used the free end to pass between my legs, up over my shoulder and back to the knot so that I was encased in a rough harness. The other end had a clip on it and I hooked it on the wire guard rail, praying that I wouldn't have to test the strength of that rail by being dragged through the water.

It took determination to leave the relative safety of the cockpit and go forward, even though I knew it had to be done. The one real danger, other than the wind shifting directly on shore and blowing us on the rocks, would be dismasting. With too much sail a strong gust might carry something away, and there would be nothing we could do after that. I kept telling myself that, but the foredeck looked awfully small and wet and was plunging around like a roller coaster.

Once I got out on it, it wasn't as bad as it had looked, of course. Things almost never are. Yet, in one way, it was worse. The soaked teak decks had got some oil spilled on them somewhere, or maybe there was some on the soles of my boots, and my feet wouldn't grip. There's only one really safe footwear on teak decks, bare feet, but in that cold I wasn't about to take my boots off. The very thought of it curled my feet into hard little balls.

The wind was rising and kept trying to tear the sail out of my hands, and the stiff salt-soaked dacron fought me like a maddened sea ray. I'd get some stuffed into the bag and the wind would blow it out again, while with just the jib and no staywail Steen was having trouble keeping his course, letting her wander off down wind, then point too high into the seas so that gray water rushed across the deck. I couldn't blame him but I could wish for a little experience at the helm while I changed sails. Eventually I got the storm staysail up and the others down and bagged, tied lines onto the sail bags and tossed them back into the cockpit, secured all the loose halyards and used the bow mooring line to lash down the spinnaker pole and boat hook. We were as ready for the gale as we'd ever be, and none too soon. The black clouds to windward were rushing down on us with their message of doom that stayed all too real despite our feeble efforts to joke about it. Intellectually I knew we were safe, in for a rough time but no worse than a lot of small-boat sailors have weathered, but it's hard to be intellectual when the ocean is so big and you're in a tiny boat. In the dark the waves looked enormous, and I thought I heard breakers now and then.

Steen did look better. The work of steering had

forced him to think about something other than his own misery. Unfortunately, the motion of the boat was getting to me now, which made me mad. I never got seasick. Well, hardly ever. But I never set out into a gale without a hot meal, wearing damp clothes and wet boots and not having enough sleep, either. I thought about dramamine, but I couldn't risk the drowsiness that comes with it. Better to be seasick than asleep, I decided. I could get the boat through the storm but Steen couldn't alone.

About midnight the real storm hit us. Until then we'd had squalls, gusts so strong the foam blew up from the sea and splattered across the deck in sheets, salt water mixed with sleet, the sky overhead as black as paint, then the wind would die away again to forty knots, letting us claw away from shore until the next one hit. Then, unexpected after we'd become used to the squalls, the wind rose to an insane fury, screaming through the rigging and heeling the boat way over until the close-hauled boom was nearly in the water. I leaped at the sail, clawing down the main and wrapping lines around it while it flapped and fought me, the wind trying to throw me off my perch on the cabin top into the dark foam all around us. After the main the storm staysail was easy, and I dragged the thick canvas back into the cockpit before stuffing it into the bag. We ran down wind under bare poles, and I prayed we had enough sea room to keep off the rocks, but we'd never do it that way. We lashed the helm to leeward, getting *Witch* to lie nearly beam on to the sea, heeled right over with the water breaking all around us. Heavy water came aboard, breaking just at the cockpit and filling it, drenching us through our oilskins as the chilly brine found its way through every opening in our clothes.

Frantically I ran below, tore through the gear in the locker under the bunks in the forepeak, found the sea anchor and bent on my heaviest mooring line, my fingers thick with cold and almost unable to tie a knot we could trust our lives to. While I was paying it out over the stern we took another breaker, and I knew we couldn't lie beam on to that sea any longer.

The sea anchor got *Witch* stern on to the seas and I lashed the tiller to port, bringing the storm onto our quarter, trying to keep out from shore as much as I could. Exactly stern on to the waves she rode easily, but as soon as we tried to work across the storm waves broke against the transom, filling the cockpit and threatening to come below. We had more sleet now, laying across the deck until everything was covered with it, a sheet of ice crystals laying there until another wave broke across us to wash it away.

The noise was unbearable. The wind set every line as taut as a violin string, and something developed a rhythmic thump! thump! that we never could find, making us wonder if the mast was coming out and conjure up imaginary disasters below the waterline. Below, the sound of water rushing past the hull was deceiving, and three or four times an hour I would lift the floorboards, looking for the leak I was sure we had developed, but each time the water level was about the same, only a little being added when we'd get another sea in the cockpit and there would be a trickle around the scupper hoses. *Witch* was doing fine, but her crew was nearly finished, our teeth chattering with cold and nervous exhaustion, every movement an agony. By four A.M. I was ready to face a dozen Pontiacs and men with guns, to fight any danger that you could shoot back at. Here we could do nothing, it had all been done. With all sail down and the sea anchor set, *Witch* drifted to leeward making about two knots toward the shore no more than ten miles away, and I couldn't tell how close the rocks were. When we'd attempt to steer away from shore we brought heavy water aboard, too much even for *Witch*'s sturdy construction. I kept the radio on, listening to weather reports, not surprised to hear that the small craft warnings had been replaced by gale warnings from Tattoosh to Cape Blanco. To make it worse, I had to have some rest. Steen didn't know how to deal with an emergency, and in my condition I couldn't. Finally I went below, leaving him out there to keep watch and try to steer between breakers, sitting proud and alone in the stern singing old Viking songs to keep awake while I tossed fitfully in the bunk. It was the longest night of our lives.

But morning came at last, a lovely day with bright sun to show us a good three miles off shore. The wind veered more north than west and drooped to forty knots. We brought in the sea anchor, turned southwest by south under storm staysail and double-reefed main, glad to see the coast drop away rapidly as *Witch* tore along at a good eight knots in the quartering wind. On our first full day at sea, despite the night we'd spent under bare poles with the sea anchor out, we made a hundred miles.

In a way it was as well that the worst was over the first night. From there south things were better. We ran into another storm off Astoria, deciding us against putting in there for supplies although I hadn't really wanted to anyway. The Columbia River mouth bar is a graveyard of ships and I wanted nothing to do with it if I could avoid it, and certainly not in a storm although the temptation to find a quiet anchorage was strong.

We ran out of beer about then, and other supplies were getting low, but I didn't have charts for the whole coast. There wasn't any real need for charts as long as I didn't put in, and we didn't see land at all, keeping fifty miles out for enough sea room to ride out anything we were likely to meet. *Witch* ran beautifully before a following wind, clipping off a hundred and forty miles a day with no strain, and with that lovely northwest wind I didn't want to run to port and lose it. Our big problem was sleep. Somebody had to be at the helm at all times, and three-hour shifts off watch just aren't long enough to get proper rest. Steen was an iron man, taking long tricks at the tiller, but I could never relax completely even though he had the helm. We learned to sleep whenever we could, the man off duty leaning against the back of the cabin, talking to the helmsman, then his chin would drop and off he'd go for a few minutes.

From what I remembered the only harbor south of the Columbia River was Crescent City until San Francisco, and the storm off Astoria carried us past that, while San Francisco was altogether too large a city to be seen in. We passed outside the Farralon Islands on the night of the sixth day, and by dawn we were off Monterey Bay. I put the helm over and headed for Carmel, easy to find without charts. There were tourists in the city, and nobody paid any attention to a couple of bearded characters in old clothes wandering through the little shops, eating at restaurants and buying groceries. Steen wanted to stay ashore for the night but I talked him out of it, and about midnight we put out to sea again, bucking the strong on-shore wind that seems to blow in that region all the time. Along the shore they have little wind-screen fences to protect the trees from it. Our course ran east of south now, taking us along highway one, which should have been great scenery if we'd been close enough to see it, but with that strong on-shore wind and fog I kept well out to sea.

I was a little nervous about rounding Point Concepcion. The Coast Pilot called it the Cape Horn of California and warned that there were always strong winds there, but it wasn't bad at all when we got to it. We took the inside channel, and nine days after we left Neah Bay, fourteen days out of Seattle, we anchored off the coast of Anacapa Island in a little protected bay off shore from the park ranger station. A couple of overnighters from the mainland were there with us and one showed altogether too much curiosity about our Washington registration number. We told him some story, I don't remember what. By that time we were ready to say the most fantastic things to people anyway.

We lay in there for two days, drying everything, cleaning up the boat, catching up on sleep, taking short cruises around the island and rowing ashore in the dinghy. We climbed the steep sides of brown parched hills and had our clothes and skin thoroughly punctured by a devil-plant cactus, a little ball of spikes that seems to jump at you. When you get one on you it sticks to whatever you use to take it off like the magical glue of the old Katzenjammer cartoons until finally you have to find something you're willing to throw away and use that. Even then if you aren't careful it will jump back on you and you have to start over.

Anacapa Island is a national monument, three hills jutting out of the sea twenty miles south of Oxnard. At high tide it is three separate islands, or as near to that as makes no difference, but you couldn't sail between them with a rowboat. Bull seals keep their harems on the lee side, and the hills are covered with devil-plant and a sunflower that looks like something that ought to grow on the moon. There is a big lighthouse at one end, with a complex of buildings, but it's been abandoned now, the light made into an automated signal. I wondered about that—with so many people unemployed in this country why do we have to eliminate the old romantic jobs? An automatic light can't throw a line to a fishing boat run on the rocks, or see a ship in trouble and radio for help, and it can't save that much money over the needs of the kind of man who would be a lighthouse keeper. Every summer the Forest Service sends dozens off to fire stations, surely we could man posts like Anacapa? It would be dignified work for a man who couldn't find anything else. But we don't and the only people on Anacapa are two rangers who have a quonset hut at the other end of the island chain.

The weather was warm, and the wind died out at night, leaving the water calm until morning when a little riffle would show, the wind slowly building up to the steady fifteen-knots northwest wind of the afternoon, dying away again at night. Our second night we were sitting below, drinking beer and feeling pleased with ourselves, when there was a flurry of splashing in the water outside followed by a clatter on deck. We rushed up to see a flying fish about eighteen inches long flopping on the foredeck. I picked it up, spread the wing fins, which looked like the webbed feet of a frog. It was really a beautiful thing. I'm told they're good to eat but this was the first one I'd ever seen, and I tossed it gently over the side, watched it swim in a furious circle leaving a bright phosphorescent trail before darting off. Every disturbance in the water produced a bright flash of light, and when the tide streamed past the anchor rope it made a silver ribbon stretching out to the depths. Chinese communists and the cold war seemed a long way away.

_8_

It was May in the Los Angeles basin, and the weather was perfect, warm gentle winds, clear skies, the water around Anacapa Island a startlingly clear blue. After three days of luxuriating with enough sleep, dry weather, and no sea duty, we set out for Catalina seventy miles to the southeast. We were under way at dawn and caught a gentle wind which took us around Anacapa and stayed with us all day, blowing stronger out of clear skies in the afternoon. We were flying all sail, the big main flattened drumtaut by the vang, our red spinnaker billowing out in front to pull us along. A school of dolphins flashed by, darting under the bows, racing along to parallel us with ease, then laughing at us and zooming far ahead, turning a great circle and flashing back directly at us, seemingly determined to ram and only changing course to miss by inches at the last second.

In the afternoon a great black fluke pounded the water a hundred yards off the bow, followed by a lazy rolling shape that seemed to go on forever before vanishing with another wave of the fluked tail. I'd never seen a whale, and I stood on the cabin, staring out where he'd been, but he never surfaced in our sight again. Catalina Island came into view in the early afternoon, a big brown shape looming up out of haze so thin that until we saw the island we'd thought the visibility perfect. We rushed along its northern shore, past the isthmus where a great wind funneled out of the gap, heeling us way over and making us laugh like schoolboys. Steen perched in the bows, one hand in the rigging and the other shading his eyes or waving as he shouted at the sea.

Close to the island the wind died away completely, and we cursed and sweated *Witch* out a few hundred yards. I was about to start the motor but Steen halted me, determined not to shatter this perfect sailing with the ugly sound of the motor, and finally we came to a thin line of riffled water, a line so sharp it might have been drawn with a brush. *Witch* heeled over, and seconds later we were out among whitecapped waves in ten knots of wind, the contrast with the still water a hundred yards away unimaginable. Catalina was a springtime splash of browns and greens rising from blue water, and it might have been Samothrace seen by the Greek warriors bound to the Trojan War. The only life in sight was sails white against the sea.

It was an hour before sundown when we sighted Casino Point which guards Avalon harbor. At first we thought it a small pavilion close up, but when we sailed on and on and it was still far away we realized that the Casino was a monstrous building, shaped like a backyard gazebo but five stories high, capped with an immense brick-red round dome. It was half an hour before we could make out the small figures of people walking around, dwarfed, at its base. There was a forest of small boats outside the point, and in Avalon harbor itself hundreds more, sailboats, power boats, little open decked catamarans that must have been sailed over from the mainland by more daring souls than I, big steam yachts a hundred feet long, and world-cruising schooners with high buff-colored masts tall above teak decks and white topsides.

We dropped the anchor just at sundown in St. Catherine's Bay, a quiet protected cove well away from the bustle of Avalon harbor, and put in the evening cooking, drinking the last of the beer from Carmel and smoking endless pipefuls of tobacco, the perfect picture of peace and contentment which couldn't last.

Mid-morning was Saturday, and I hailed the shore-boat, leaving Steen aboard. Avalon was a long street of shops and bars and restaurants, open-air hot dog stands and artists displaying their paintings on the low wall separating the beach from the streets. No cars were allowed along the beach area, but people walked on the sidewalks anyway, conditioned to the mechanical tyranny of the true masters of our civilization. It was hard to shake the idyllic mood, but I found a telephone booth and dialed the number I'd carefully carried with me all the way from Seattle.

"Airport marina," it answered from the mainland twenty miles away.

"Miss Carruthers, Ann Carruthers, please." After a moment there was another ring, a second, a long moment of doubt.

"Yes."

"It's D-day all over again. The marines have landed," I told Janie.

"Darling—are you all right?"

"Of course I'm all right. What could happen to me? You can tell your friends that all's well, home is the sailor, home from the sea, and the hunter home from the hill." The last was an identification code. Corny or not I'd chosen it myself, and it didn't seem out of place.

She wanted to ask me where I was, but she was too well trained for that. "I've got a couple of days before I'm due at the next place. Where can we meet?"

I thought about that for a second. Without prior arrangements there aren't too many places to put a sailboat in Los Angeles, or at least so I'd been told. I'd need Janie's help, and it seemed a long way from the back roads near Carnation. "Take the steamer to Avalon harbor. I'll meet you in a place called The Attic for dinner tonight. Bring some overnight things . . . bring your swimsuit too. Only I'd rather we didn't tell the man where, if you can get away with that."

"Ha. I know you, trying to get me back in your clutches again. . . . It sounds wonderful, I'll be there. We won't be noticed?"

"No." The whole beach was covered with couples, not many wedding rings in sight. I was more conspicuous without a girl, although with her legs Janie certainly wouldn't vanish in the crowd. "I'll be waiting for you, sweetheart. Nothing says we can't have a couple of days' vacation before we get back in the grind."

"I'll be there." She blew me a kiss over the telephone, and I went off to buy groceries and beer.

Our vacation lasted two days. We swam in the surf, rowed around Avalon harbor in the dinghy, sat on deck and watched the tides churn the rocky beach out where we were anchored, each wave lifting the gravel and making a rushing sound as it ground the rocks together. In a thousand years it would all be sand. We didn't have a thousand years.

Monday night we sat in the cabin of a big Chris-Craft anchored fifty yards from us. Sunday afternoon the pleasure boat fleet had all disappeared toward Los Angeles, leaving St. Catherine's to us, and Monday afternoon the cruiser appeared in response to Janie's telephone call. We rowed over after dark, climbed on board to find Harry Shearing sitting at the dinette, his inevitable Camels and coffee in front of him. The cabin of the boat looked like a ballroom after the cramped quarters in *Witch*.

Shearing nodded judiciously, studying me. "One thing to be said for your transportation, Crane. It changes the appearance. I'd never have recognized either one of you."

He was probably right. I'd kept smooth shaven, but the sun had bleached my hair almost white, burned my face to a dark tan with almost white eyebrows. Steen had kept his whiskers, now sported a short neatly trimmed beard that grew at a fantastic rate. We looked like a couple of beach bums. "OK, what's the drill?" I asked.

Shearing grinned. "Anxious to get back to work? Sit down, have a drink. I want you to meet Sam." He indicated a short swarthy man with a round almost Asiatic face a deeper bronze than even mine was. "Sam de la Torres, my senior agent in this area. Meet Paul Crane, Sam."

De la Torres looked at me critically, measuring me thoughtfully before he put out his hand. "A pleasure, señor." The accent wasn't strong, but it was there. He'd never pass for anything but a chicano. Shearing introduced him to Janie and Steen, and we all sat around the dinette, the picture of lucky stiffs who could vacation on weekdays.

"We've looked into those people in Seattle," Shearing said. "Definitely hired talent. We let them lay and right now the Washington police are wondering if there's a gang war going on in their territory. Leaves a puzzle for whoever sent the button men. Your car has been discreetly repaired, by the way."

"Thanks. Any idea of who sent them?"

"No." Shearing lit another cigarette, offered the pack around without takers. "But that kind of interest moves your operation up to a little more prominence, which is why I've decided to work out of L.A. for a while. We've got somebody worried. Eventually we'll find out who."

I laughed. I didn't point out that I could get used up in the finding out. He knew that anyway.

"The Bureau had an anonymous tip," Shearing added. "We're fairly sure of that. Crane, you have officially been in Montana helping the Air Force solve some problems with frost upheavals in their Minuteman base. The Bureau may apologize for searching your house when you get back. On the other hand, they may just forget the whole thing and hope you never find out they were in there."

"It's nice to be unwanted," I said.

"Yeah. But it wouldn't be a good idea to come to their attention just now. One of their people might remember your name. The last thing I need is to have the Bureau running around in circles in L.A., and they're mad as hell about losing Steen. None of their people are in on this so watch out. Now. We've got to get you back in circulation. Janie can't stay out of sight any longer, her friends in Information Associates might begin to wonder just who she works for. Despite your suspicions of my office, I think it safe to assume that the leak to the Bureau and whoever hired those Seattle enforcers must have come from an information salesman, which gives us a small problem. If we put Dr. Hoorne out where everybody can see him, what's to prevent this from happening again?"

"Not much," Steen muttered.

"Right," Shearing agreed. "So we won't put you out where they can see you. We'll put Crane out there."

"We will, eh?" I asked.

"Certainly. That attack was hardly directed at you. It's reasonable to assume that someone doesn't want Dr. Hoorne to sell his information, and that they don't really care how they prevent it. What interest would they have in Paul Crane?''

I nodded. "I came to the same conclusion on the way down here. It's got to be Steen they want dead or alive. But who gains from putting him out of circulation?''

Shearing shook his head. "It is a puzzle, but not our main problem at the moment. We have to put Dr. Hoorne in a safe house and establish our contacts with the information people again. It's too bad Janie can't get them to trust her with the name of the Chinese agent they deal with, but we were certain they wouldn't. I don't see any alternative but to go on with the plan despite the complications.''

"It may be complex indeed, señor,'' de la Torres said. He was standing by the helmsman's seat, a duplicate to the flying bridge above the cabin. With his little blue yachting cap and striped pullover sweater he looked quite at home on a boat, even though you don't normally think of the Spanish as seafaring people. That's silly, of course, they were putting out of Cadiz into the ocean back when most people thought the world was flat, and although we hear more about the military exploits of the Conquistadores than we do about their navy, they weren't too bad at the exploration business. The name of the Straits of Juan de Fuca as well as the names of all the islands and cities along the California coast proved that.

"What I mean,'' he continued, "is this. Once it becomes known that Dr. Hoorne is in this area, we must assume that the Bureau will be informed as well. They will search for him quite vigorously, and when they learn, as it must be supposed they will, that Señor Crane is the contact with Dr. Hoorne, Crane will be watched.''

"They might try to hire some more enforcers, too," Janie added. "We're putting Paul into quite a dangerous situation."

"He's in no danger until they locate Hoorne," Shearing said. "Until then he's no threat to anybody. The Bureau won't have any grounds to arrest him. However, I will fix it up with the Montana outfit to say Paul finished his assignment and is taking a well-earned vacation in southern California." He gritted his teeth. "It's always a mess dealing with a leaky outfit like that Information Associates. The hell of it is we don't even know if they've got one leak or two."

I nodded. "You mean they may have a Bureau plant in there. . . ."

"And whoever it was that hired the enforcers. Or it may be the same person. Either way, I think we have to help Information Associates plug up their leaks."

"The Bureau will not care much for that," de la Torres said. He wasn't objecting, just pointing it out. "It will not be easy. I do not have very many men to work with here. Perhaps you should tell me as much as you know about this group."

Shearing nodded to Janie. "Brief him."

She put her fingers to her lips for a second, concentrating on where to begin. "The leader of the group is a very young man named Jim Vallery. He calls himself Dick when he's dealing with outsiders, and he's very bright. I understand he has almost a doctorate in physics from Johns Hopkins, but he didn't finish his thesis work. Background check shows that he was drafted, chose OCS, and after he was commissioned went into the technical branches of the army. He did so well that they sent him to graduate school at Johns Hopkins, but when he got to thinking about how long he'd have to stay in the army as part of their agreement to send him to school, he flunked all his courses just before he would have to graduate, finished his hitch, and was discharged. He's quite bitter about the military, and seems to be sincere in believing in some kind of theory of absolute freedom.''

Steen nodded. ''That is the one we met. I can tell you he is very knowledgeable about theoretical physics, although he has little practical experience and does not know the details of the latest research. I agree with Janie, a very bright young man indeed.''

''Next,'' Shearing prompted.

''Beverly Henderson. Graduate of the University of Oregon, majored in liberal arts. Two years younger than Vallery, twenty-three. Sort of a phony intellectual attitude about everything. She's very attached to Vallery, would marry him in an instant, but his particular theory of society has it that marriage is a form of slavery and he's having none of it. She lives with him and makes the best of what she's got, but she doesn't like it. I heard her yelling at him once, about how his theories were wonderful, but why was it that he always got what he wanted and she didn't.'' Janie made a face, but whether she meant this was typical of men, or something else, I couldn't tell. ''She's got money, an allowance. Her old man owns about half of Oregon and a lot of California including some oil fields near Bakersfield. She claims to believe this ultra-free enterprise theory of Vallery's, but when she's away from him she doesn't come on so strong with it. I think most of it's put on, and what she mainly believes in is her boy friend. She likes excitement too, but she's getting scared— I don't think she likes his new line of work very much.''

''Does she dislike it enough to be willing to save him from treason at the cost of hiring murder done?'' de la Torres asked.

''I don't know, Sam. Vallery's sold some papers and things already, enough to put him in jail, but it might be hard to prove in court. This is the biggest

deal they've had and they could all go away for a
long time if they were caught. It's possible, but I
never thought of it."

Sam nodded sleepily, leaned back against the controls. Janie looked thoughtful for a second, consider-
ing the idea for the first time. It obviously appealed
to her. She chewed on it a while, then went on with
the briefing. "The other scientist I've met is Dr.
Prufro. He was pretty well known once but he left
the atomic laboratories at Sandia after a big fight
with the director and got himself a position at Cal
Tech. He didn't stay more than a year, and Cal Tech
doesn't want him back. He got involved with one of
his students. The funny thing is that he was apparently in love with her; her parents complained when
he kept after her after she was through the affair.

"Prufro's a rabbity sort of guy most of the time,
but there's a stubborn streak in him. I guess falling
for young girls is normal for him, because now he's
nuts about Beverly Henderson. He wants her so bad
he can't hide it, but all he can do is moon about it.
It's so obvious that Jim Vallery once threatened to
beat him to a pulp, but then Vallery's theories got in
his way and he apologized for being possessive and
irrational. It really upset Bev—she liked having Jim
come on like a jealous lover. She's teased Prufro, led
him on trying to get that reaction out of Vallery
again, but no luck." Janie gave a little grin of sympathy with Bev, thought better of it, and reached
across the table for Shearing's Camels, lit one
although she usually likes the filtered variety. This
started a chain reaction, Steen and I on our pipes,
Shearing with another Camel.

"Those are the main people. There are a couple of
secondary troops. Sharon Culver, light brown hair,
five four or so, slim boyish figure, very young face.
She ropes in people with information, same as me.
She's pretty good with the roping, but Vallery's con-

science gets in the way when it's time to put the screws in. She's hooked some guy who works out of Los Angeles but spends his time in Colorado Springs, he's panting after her and his wife would kill him if she found out. Prufro wants to tell the guy to kick through with the information or they go to the wife, but Vallery's held off. The group's all desperate for money, they spent a lot setting it up and not much has come in. A good bit of the pressure for money comes from a weasely little creep named Bert Facks who's supposed to know about airplane design. He looks more like a hood to me. I know he carries a gun. He's always after them to close this Colorado Springs deal.''

"Facks," Shearing mused. "We weren't able to get anything on him. His prints are not on file with the Bureau and the photograph you were supposed to take could not be developed. He is here in Los Angeles, you say?''

She nodded. "I saw him in Seattle, but not much. I think he travels. Look, it wasn't my fault the picture didn't come out.''

Shearing winked at her. "I didn't say it was. It's still a pity we can't identify the elusive Mister Facks, but we'll take care of that in time. Who's left?''

"None that I know in the Los Angeles area. There are the Hedder brothers, Joe and John, up in Seattle. It was through Joe Hedder that I got to Vallery. They're runners, they watched Paul's house, things like that.''

"Surely there must be more involved than that," de la Torres insisted. "There must be someone in Los Angeles beside the girl Sharon.''

Janie nodded. "I agree, but I haven't met anyone else.''

"Which one has the contact with the Chinese?" de la Torres asked. "That is the one we must watch, and I have very few men.''

"Jim Vallery," Janie said. "I'm not sure anyone else knows a thing about the contact. Sometimes I get the impression that they're all waiting for Vallery to let them know who the buyers are so they can take over themselves, but I haven't any reason for it. Anyway Vallery's smart enough to know that his contact with the buyers is the only thing he's really got, and he's careful."

"It is not much to work with," de la Torres said. He spread his hands, then gave a broad smile. "Of course I have often had to work with less, but it would be pleasant to have something definite for a change. Ah, well, we still do the best we can."

Shearing nodded. "I haven't seen anything to make us change the original plan. We get Janie to the Hollywood Roosevelt and wait for them to make contact. She puts them in touch with Paul and she's out of the picture for a while. We won't let them know where Paul is, just arrange a meeting so that he can be satisfied that the deal's safe, and we keep Steen out of sight until he's got it set up." Shearing ran his fingers across the dinette top. A chart of the coast from Concepcion to San Diego was laminated in plastic on the table, and he traced various courses through the islands, ending with the Catalina-to-L.A. run. "You're going to be hard to satisfy, Paul. You've been shot at, turned in to the FBI, scared half to death, and you're mad as hell. That shouldn't be hard for you to put on. You want to see money, and nothing moves until you see it in large quantities. They'll have to drag out their buyer to save the deal." He stared at the chart for a second, then turned to de la Torres.

"Sam, you cover Paul, but don't risk being seen. He should be safe enough until he's got Dr. Hoorne out in the open. And stay away from Vallery, but I want every local agent we can shake loose to stand by for the shadow job when the meet finally is set up. Along those lines, I've got a few suggestions that ought to interest you. . . . Is there any more coffee on this tub? This could take the rest of the night.''

It didn't, but it was midnight before Shearing took Steen away on the power boat, leaving Janie and me alone together for the first time since Seattle. We sat on deck watching the cruiser vanish into the dark. Behind us was a deserted beach, the nearest boat in the anchorage a big ninety foot schooner a hundred yards away. After the Chris-Craft was gone there was nothing but bright stars and a glow to the northeast, the lights of Los Angeles twenty miles away, nearly invisible in the thin mist and smog over that way. The sky above us was clear, showing every star and constellation, and we tried to see the patterns the ancients had seen, the bears and dogs and the rest of them.

"They had better imaginations than I do," Janie said. "Hercules doesn't look like a man, just a lot of stars." I pointed out the Scorpion way to the south, but she had trouble making it out.

"They didn't have much else to do but watch stars, I guess," I told her. "I can't figure out most of them, but I've had to learn to recognize constellations to find stars for navigation." I stood and yawned elaborately, my insides a tight ball of anticipation which I was trying to hide. "It's getting wet out here, girl, we better get below."

"I suppose. I could use some coffee, anyway." She stood with me in the little cockpit, then moved against me, her arm lightly around my waist. The boat rocked gently in the tide, and we stood like that. "We have to leave this and get to work in the morning," she sighed. "I wish we didn't. It's very peaceful out here."

I held her to me, thinking about what she'd said. "There's nothing making us go in tomorrow. Except we said we'd do it."

"That's enough, isn't it? You don't like this work, Paul. Why?"

"I don't know. Come on, let's get below before we drown." The dew was forming fast, as it always does on cool nights after warm days on the water. It seemed thicker than usual, and a little strange, dew dripping off the furled sails in a clear night. Below it was snug and warm, the little kerosene lights giving a cheery yellow glow that electricity can't ever match on a boat.

"It's got to be done," she insisted. "And aren't you interested in fighting back? They would have killed you if they could."

"Sure, Janie." I started to fuss with the stove. She reminded me of warrior women, and remembering the girls in the picket lines on both sides of our youthful rebellions, I wondered if most of our male fighting spirit had been killed off in the wars, leaving us only our women. I lit the stove and turned to her. "Look, I'm no soft-hearted idiot. I know it's got to be done. And it isn't that I'm too scared to do it, although I admit I get just as scared as the next guy. I just wish we could do it some other way." She started to say something, but I cut her off. "And don't tell me how impossible that is, I know it already. Look, Janie, I'm the sort of guy who likes to play things by the rules. Now the other side doesn't admit there are any rules, and we have to toss out our rulebook or lose. OK. So we do it. And it looks like I'm in the fight, and I better learn there's no umpire and get with the dirty tricks. So I'm learning, and I didn't say I'd get out of the game, but I don't have to like it."

She sat on one of the bunks, lay back against the cushions, her hair tangled from the wind and mist outside, lipstick long since chewed off in the conference with Shearing. She didn't look anything like the immaculate creature I'd taken to the dance at the Casino two nights before. Her very practical and very baggy sailing slacks were rumpled, her deck shoes stained with salt water, the scarf she'd put over her hair didn't do a thing for her, and she was a hell of a lot lovelier than she'd been the first day I saw her in her bank executive outfit. I reached for the coffeepot, and she said, "I don't really want any coffee, Paul. We have to get an early start in the morning, and after we get to Los Angeles we're back in that game you don't like. . . . Does your rule book say anything about what the players do the night before another inning?"

I started to answer, but it was easier to show her. About an hour later we realized that I'd left the damn stove burning, and I had to get up to shut it off.

9

THEY'D PUT ME in the Royal Inn in Santa Monica. I understand there are more Royal Inns around the country, all just like this one, which is a frightening thought. My Royal Inn was a steel-and-glass tower built like an office building, with non-load-bearing walls between rooms, a false cellotex ceiling hanging on metal straps, and the rest of the low-cost tricks designers are using nowadays. Outside was the usual postage-stamp-sized swimming pool, and beyond that was a parking lot bigger than the hotel. They hadn't screened off the pool from the parking lot so that the bathers had to lie around in the sun with the headlights of civilization's real masters staring at them. Some of the modern cars at least had the decency to close their eyes.

The place had a bar called the Lost Knight, which they'd tried to give some character with the decorations, but the efficiency experts had got there before the bartender. When I went in for a beer in the middle of the afternoon the stereo was pouring out some fertility rite beat at a decibel level that made it impossible to sit there, chasing me back out but they wouldn't let me take my beer. The lobby doubled as a communications hall from the front to the back of the place, with a little registration desk stuck off to one side and no space for anyone to sit. I suppose all hotels will eventually be like this one, and there are probably people who'll insist that this is a perfectly valid style for our modern age; the frightening thought is they may be right. They'll point out how convenient it is to have ice and coke machines on each floor so the guests don't have to call room service, and they'll be partly right, although with so many people unemployed it's a little strange to believe that personal services are priced out of the market. They'll tell you how convenient self-service elevators are. They'll tell you that cornice pieces and elaborate trim spoil the lines of our clean true and good architecture, and maybe they'll be right. But what they won't want to admit is that we don't have any choice anymore. Our age is the age of the cheap and shoddy because we haven't the money, the time, or the skilled workmen to make anything else.

My room was decent-sized, which should have made me grateful. A lot of the really colorful old hotels have rooms you could put handles on and use for coffins. I was on the second floor. My outside wall was all glass, sliding panels with a balcony fully a foot wide extending beyond them so I could step more or less outside and enjoy a view of the muscle crowd on the beach a block away. Since my balcony was about two feet higher than the white-gravel-covered flat roof of the lower floor box extending out from under the tower construction of the hotel, the iron railing they'd given me to keep me from falling to my death was a little superfluous, but all the other stories had iron rails on their balconies so we second-story people got them too. Looking south I couldn't see the marina where we'd put *Witch of Endor*, but she was there, all her gear stowed below and locked away because Los Angeles isn't a safe place to leave a boat unlocked. In my old moorage near the house-boats in Seattle I'd never locked up.

I'd unpacked my junk and was about to go out for some beer I could drink in quiet when the phone rang. "There is a message waiting for you when you get to the Hollywood Roosevelt," Janie told me after we'd gone through the identification routines and we were both sure nobody was holding a gun on either one of us. Shearing had worked out some clever contingency codes to use for various situations, and I hoped I could remember them all.

"What's the skinny?" I asked her.

"They want a meeting as soon as possible. Tonight."

"Aw, there goes dinner. I noticed an Indonesian place about a block from here, I was planning to feed you an eighteen-course rijsttafel tonight."

"It will have to wait, but that's sweet of you to think of it . . . what's 'rize staffel,' anyway?"

"It means rice table. You start with rice and add on various things. Curried oranges, chicken, beef, sweet and sour vegetables, fried bananas . . . you name it, they've thought of it. This place seems pretty genuine. Well, we have a chance some other time. Can you arrange the deal for tonight?"

"Yes. They seemed anxious, so I already did, subject to confirmation with you. At eight tonight you're to get to the Santa Monica Mall at Wilshire, walk along the Mall until you come to Broadway and go down Broadway to the beach. Go south on the beach until somebody meets you."

"That sounds pretty cagey . . . they scared of something?"

"I think so. And all they'll do tonight is make contact. Look, the way they've got this set up, de la Torres can't cover you very closely. They obviously picked this method so that they can see if anyone is following you."

"I'll manage. Will Sam's boys be somewhere around?"

"He'll try to be there, but he says you can't count on him to move in very fast if anything happens. As long as Dr. Hoorne's still hidden nobody thinks you're in danger, but be careful, darling."

"I'll just do that . . . well, I'll see you later. Wait a second, remembered something. I've got half your chemistry laboratory here. You left it in my bag."

"Now you know all my girlish secrets. I'll get it later. Bye, Paul."

"Goodbye, sweetheart." I hung up the phone and contemplated the junk I'd been talking about. It was a little disillusioning. I mean, if a girl had to take that many bottles and spray cans to a weekend on Catalina, what did she usually have with her, and how much of what you see is girl and how much was bought in the drug store? But then I had good reason to know she looked all right without external aids. When we'd gone dancing on the Island she'd put on the whole bit, pancake goop and the rest of it, but she looked better on the boat the last night.

I stacked the junk in one corner of the big bureau and the hell with what the chambermaid thought, although that might be interesting. . . . Nowadays when the hotel staff sees girl makeup in a man's room, do they assume he has a girlfriend or that he uses it himself? One can was hairspray and from the label it ought to be handled like an atom bomb. It cautioned me that the junk was flammable under high pressure, and under no circumstances should I puncture the can, incinerate it, or otherwise dispose of it carelessly, leaving me to wonder just what you were supposed to do with it after you were through. Eventually I got unpacked and went out on an unsuccessful search for a quiet place to have a beer.

The Santa Monica Mall is a nice development, and

proof that men can sometimes triumph over the automobile. They've closed off a street, bricked it over, and put in potted trees and things like that so that people can walk without having to worry about being run over. However, you still have to cross streets at each block, showing that the AAA had influence in the city council.

I walked along, looking at shops and trying to keep from turning around to spot a familiar face. I wasn't supposed to be watching for Information Associates, or for Sam de la Torres either. I wondered if he'd be there. His main job was protecting Steen, who was stashed away in a miserable frame house in Venice, one of those old places built in the twenties or before when Venice had canals. Now it was surrounded by similar houses cut up into ten apartments each and inhabited by bearded beach boys and the shapeless girls with stringy hair who seem to congregate down there.

Santa Monica is only a couple of miles north of Venice, but the atmosphere is entirely different. In Santa Monica the beach crowd looks more like Jones Beach. I suppose the police make life difficult for the hairy people with rope-soled shoes. Still, Santa Monica is a strange place. The people resent being part of Los Angeles and blame all their weirdies on Angelenos creeping in to use their beaches, but they've got some of their own. For example, the gentleman on the bicycle. Now bicycles are a great means of transportation and good exercise, and Eisenhower's heart specialist had a big campaign on a few years back to get us all out pedaling madly around the countryside, but this chap would stand out in a crowd of bicyclers. He was about fifty, a fat man with a round English face, wearing a spotless white turtleneck, white gloves, and black bowler hat. He'd been riding hard, but there was no sweat dripping down his ruddy cheeks; it wouldn't dare. His machine was high and boxy, one of the old-time bikes you see in circuses. He kept his head up so high he couldn't see the streets, pedaling along like a proper gentleman ignoring the peasants to either side.

He rolled down Broadway past me, stopping for a red light, not in obedience to the mechanical signal but because he *wanted* to stop just there and then. At the light there was another character. This one was flabby and bronze-faced in jeans and red-checkered shirt, green suspenders, a kid's shiny silver marshal's badge pinned on a filthy brown vest so much too small for him that his shirt and braces showed under it. He mopped his face with a red bandana, and with his other hand he was holding a long hunting horn made out of a Texas steerhorn with a bugle mouthpiece stuck in the small end. He stood on an accommodation bench at the bus stop with the horn jammed in his mouth. The bench was placed there courtesy of the Zimmelmeyer One-Stop Funeral Home, shaded by a big palm tree.

Every now and then this guy would stick the horn to his lips and give a long mournful toot for no reason I could see unless he was Zimmelmeyer and this was a special service. He practically put the thing in the highminded cyclist's ear and blew his head off, causing the gentleman bikeman to pedal madly down the street, still looking neither to the right nor to the left.

Those were typical samples of the sights around my part of Santa Monica. Walking south, the expensive hotels and new crackerboxes like the Royal Inn gave way to a mixture with run-down old beach houses thrown in, but there were still plenty of the modern efficiency hotels like the Royal, where every square inch of space was scientifically used—the designers would say utilized—giving it the atmosphere of an aerospace think tank. Maybe that was deliber-

ate; Rand Corporation, the original think tank where
we keep the tame geniuses who are going to save us
from both war and pollution was only about a block
away from the Royal Inn.

It was early evening, and couples strolled along the
walk by the water in the twilight. Fifty to a hundred
yards of littered sand separated us from the surf,
which was making spectacular breakers against the
shore. I walked south until I'd left just everybody
behind, strolling along the deserted promenade and
feeling a hell of a temptation to look over my shoulder, stop and tie my shoes, anything to try to see if
anybody was interested in me, but I fought it down.

About a mile south of the Mall, a girl came out of
the shadows and fell in beside me. "Hello, Paul,"
she said as if we'd known each other for years.

"Hello, Bev. You the one I'm supposed to meet?"

"No. Ji—I mean, Dick will be along. He's watching us to see you weren't followed."

"You look great," I told her.

"Why thank you." She took my hand, which was
a surprise, although it did make us less noticeable.
"But I didn't really try, you know."

"No. That's just it." She was wearing a little tan
and red miniskirted one-piece dress with some kind
of footwear that had no toes but extended halfway
up her calves. Her white leather coat was thrown over
her shoulders like a cape. She had a couple of bright
colored scarves tied into her hair so that most of it
came down over her right shoulder and curled under
her face. "After all the stringy hair and unwashed
clothes I've seen today on the beach and the Mall,
you're ready to take the grand prize. I don't know
why young American girls go to so much trouble to
look ugly, but they make it. They look like ugly little
kids." We caught sight of one, dirty bare feet slap-
ping along the sand, jeans with bottoms two feet
wide flapping in time with them, a shapeless white

upper garment that might have been a man's shirt and might have been anything else. Fixed up she would have looked all right. "She looks like somebody hit her with an uglystick."

"Be quiet, she'll hear you," Bev giggled.

"She ought to. When I get to be dictator, I'm going to pass a rule. Any girl appears in public looking ugly like that, men have a right to kick her. One kick per girl per man per day, we don't want to stomp any of them to death, just encourage them to stop polluting our cities."

Bev giggled again, looked back over her shoulder.

"You're not supposed to do that," I told her. "Very bad technique. Anyway, why all the mystery? You have reason to be scared?"

"You know we do. We read the Seattle papers. What happened on the road after you met us in Carnation?"

"I was wondering if you knew anything about that. After all, you people picked the meeting place and told us which way to drive away from it. Sure they weren't yours?"

She drew away from me. "Why would we do that. It wasn't us, Paul. But—but what did happen? The papers said two men were shot out there on the road. Did you shoot them?"

"What makes you think we had anything to do with it?"

"Well, it would be a funny coincidence. . . . I mean, Seattle doesn't have gang warfare, and you were there when it happened."

I nodded. "A couple of guys thought we'd look good in their car. We didn't agree."

"Did you—did you kill them?"

"Come on, Bev. Let's talk about something else. I'm not admitting anything like that."

"But—but who were they?" As we talked she led me up a side street away from the water, off into a jungle of houses and hamburger stands. From there we walked through deserted side streets and alleys, twisting around until I knew nobody would be able to follow us. I wasn't even sure where I was myself.

"I sort of hoped you might know who they were," I told her. "Well, I guess there's just a lot of occupational risk to this business." I didn't feel as tough as I talked. There were occupational hazards to the whole situation, and I was uneasily aware that de la Torres had probably lost me, if he'd been there at all. I was on my own. The Luger felt good in my belt, and I moved my hand over my shirt to feel it through the cloth.

We came to a little park and sat on a bench. She moved against me, for appearance I guessed, but it was disturbing. It bothered me more than it ought to have. Here I was convincing myself that I was doing this mainly for Janie, talking myself into being in love with her. I shouldn't be thinking about how nice this kid looked in her short skirt, or how warm she felt against me in the evening chill. Still, it would have been hard to ignore Bev. She wasn't exactly trying to be ignored.

I wondered if she liked the situation too, since there was nobody around to put the show on for. I found myself wondering if this could develop into something, and if I wanted it to. At the same time the working part of my brain laughed like hell.

"How'd you get in this crummy game?" I asked her. "You need the money that bad?"

She started to laugh, but then got real serious. "No. We don't need it at all. But that's a strange question for you to ask, isn't it?"

"Not really. I do need the money. I don't have to like what I'm doing to get it, do I? Besides, I can tell myself if I didn't help arrange for the other side to get what they want, somebody else would. They don't seem to have much trouble, from what I read our scientific outfit is shot through with spies. This country has never been much good at secrecy." I was getting real good at explaining myself to girls. Just last night I was giving a similar line to Janie.

"You need money . . . how much do you need, Paul? What would it take to get you out of this?"

"I never thought. Is that a serious offer?"

"Yes. I'm scared, Paul. Dick's got us involved in something that's just too big, and I'm scared. They —they executed the Rosenbergs."

"Sure they did. I doubt that you can remember that far back. I wasn't too old when it happened myself, and I'm older than you."

"I can read. And things are getting ugly in this country, people are getting mad. . . . I don't want Dick mixed up in it. How much will you take? I can't pay any hundred thousand dollars, but I could . . . I could get you ten thousand. For nothing. You wouldn't have to commit any crimes, and if that's not enough, I could make it interesting for you in other ways, too." She moved against me, a suggestion of what she had in mind.

"What good would that do? Even if you got out, your boyfriend would still be a spy."

"He's not a spy!" she protested. "We—oh, Lord, it's too complicated to explain. But if this deal falls through, I think he's scared enough to drop out. Think about it, Paul. You wouldn't have to do anything, and—and it might be a lot of fun." She leaned over and kissed me on the mouth, hard, her body alive against mine, her hands moving over me. Her lips were soft, gentle, and I felt my arms tighten around her without my thinking about it . . . finally *I* broke away.

"I can have a lot of fun with my part of a million bucks," I said harshly. I was almost out of breath. "And I've already got a girl."

"You think you have," she said. "You mean that Janie Youngs, don't you? Well, she's not your girl, Paul. She works for Information Associates, and her only interest in you is the money you're going to get. You might not get any money at all, and I'm offering you ten thousand dollars any time you want to take it. Isn't that better than a chance of getting killed? Or going to jail? With ten thousand you should be able to start over somewhere, you said you didn't like this very much anyway, and you've already made a lot of money out of it." She talked very fast, and she hadn't moved away from me at all.

I heard noises behind us and figured it was Jim Vallery. I wasn't sorry to have him come, it was getting tough to hold her away even if I knew she wasn't really interested in me, only in persuading me to help her save Vallery. You can always believe that the girl will fall for you if things go far enough. . . . Besides, I was running out of excuses that didn't make me sound like a moneymad traitor, and I didn't like her thinking that of me. When Bev heard him she moved guiltily away from me. "Don't tell him I mentioned Janie," she warned. "But you think about what I told you, and, and, about what happened here."

"Nobody followed you," Vallery said from behind us. "Let's get this over with."

"Suits me," I told him. "You said come to L.A., we're here. No thanks to those jokers out on the Carnation road. You sure you don't know who they were?"

"No, of course not. Where is Dr. Hoorne? You were supposed to bring him with you."

"You were supposed to bring money, too. You got it? Show me money and I'll produce Steen."

He sat on the bench with us, and Bev moved over toward him, not sitting as close as she had with me. She kept looking at me with a pleading look. Hell, I wasn't about to tell Vallery she'd offered me money, and more, to call off the deal, although she'd never guess the reason I wouldn't.

"You really mean it," he said. "You actually want to see the money."

"Damn betcha. I want to know you've got it to pay with. Look, Mister, we've got something to sell. Not give away, sell. You claim you can buy it, but I'm not real sure of that. You're convenient, but don't kid me that I can't wander out into L.A. and find a contact of my own. It might take me some time, and there's risk involved, but I'd do it if I had to. I'd say it was about time you got off the dime and earned some of that fancy cut you think you're going to get. Come up with the stakes, Dick, or get out of the game."

"I was told by our buyer that that's a lot of money." He wasn't particularly impressed by my hard-case act.

"So we haggle over the price. Or knock some out of your cut. Look, buddy, you got your free sample. Now when do we see some money so I know I'm not wasting my time?"

"Tomorrow," he said grimly. "Bring Dr. Hoorne here tomorrow afternoon at three and we'll take you to the money, both of you."

I stood up, shaking my head. "Look, how many times do I have to tell it? No money, no Steen. You show me money, I show you Hoorne. And pick your place carefully, Mister. No dark alleys. No lonely beaches. We're taking no chances on you people picking up Steen and keeping the money."

"All right. Be here tomorrow. But you better be able to produce him, Crane. After all you've put us through, this better not fizzle out. They won't let you live through a doublecross."

"Yeah." As I walked away I thought there was a good chance they wouldn't let me live even if I didn't try a doublecross. If they got Steen, why would they need me?

10

I WALKED THROUGH a maze of alleyways to the more inhabited streets, made a few excursions off my direct route just for the fun of it, and headed back to my hotel. I thought somebody might be behind me, probably de la Torres or his troops, but I didn't worry about losing them. He'd find me easily enough.

The evening had been a waste of time, but I'd expected that. Vallery wanted to make one more try without producing the money. Now he'd have to go to his buyer. I hoped Vallery could talk him into it. If he could, this whole thing would be over in a day or so, and Janie and I could go back to Seattle. Thinking about that got me to worrying about *Witch of Endor*. She'd have to be trucked, I sure as hell wasn't going to sail a boat *up* that coast against the prevailing winds. As I walked along, I gave some thought to the problem of a wooden boat out of the water on a truck. In that warm climate, she'd dry out fast and the seams would open up.

I wanted a drink, but the noise level in the Lost Knight was worse than ever. They had a combo of some kind in there, with a character who seemed determined to swallow the mike wailing about his long-lost love, or maybe it was his dog that was lost. I gave up on the Lost Knight and entered the elevator. A couple of little girls got off as it came down to the lobby, pretty little teenagers in skirts and low-heeled shoes, chattering in Japanese, although I don't think I'd noticed they were Oriental until I heard them talking, they looked so Western. The way our teenagers dress, the typical Western-looking kids will all be foreigners in a few years.

A couple of guys made a rush for the elevator and I held it for them. After the doors closed I pushed the button for two, then, when they made no move to the controls, looked at them. One of them had a knife which he pushed against my ribs.

"Be very quiet, Mr. Crane," he said. "Keep your hands out where we can see them, and act natural. If you attract any attention, I will kill you."

"Sure." I tried to do what he wanted. The Luger in my belt seemed a good fifty miles away with that knife in my back. The elevator doors opened and they walked along with me, saying something about how nice it was to run into me here. "Which room is yours, Paul?" the knife artist asked for the benefit of the beefy character getting ice out of the machine by the elevator.

"It's down here." They were behind me, and I hadn't had a very good look at them. From what I remembered they were just average-looking guys, although the one with a knife had a flat face that might have been partly Oriental. It might have been Slavic for that matter. The other one was shorter and skinny with pointed features. "Who are you?" I asked.

"You will say nothing more," he said. He emphasized it with a little poke with the knife, not enough to hurt but it let me know it was still there, if I needed reminding.

"I'll have to put my hand in my pocket to get the key," I warned him.

"Just be very careful. Take it out slowly, that's good. Is this the room?"

"Yeah." I put the key in and opened the door, hoping that de la Torres might be inside waiting. I stepped in quickly, prepared to throw myself on the floor if he was, but there was nobody there at all.

"One moment, Carl," the knife man said. He reached around, patted my middle, and took the Luger out of my belt, stuck it into his own. "Now, check the bathroom and closets."

Carl looked around, shook his head. "Nothing here, Frank."

"Look carefully to see if there are any clothes belonging to anyone besides Mr. Crane."

Carl poked around in my bags, went through the closets. "Nope. It looks like it's all his stuff, barring that junk on the bureau." He indicated Janie's chemistry laboratory.

"But no female clothing. Well, we have time. Mr. Crane can explain it all to us. First, where is Dr. Hoorne?"

"Who?" I asked.

He hit me. It was a good hard punch, his fist catching me in the side of the back just above the belt, right over the kidney. I felt weak, my knees stopped wanting to hold me up, and I had to catch the bureau to keep from falling. "We are not here to play games, Mr. Crane. You are going to tell us where Dr. Hoorne is, and you are going to tell us a great many other things. Make no mistake about that. The only uncertainty is what will happen to you before you tell us. If you are cooperative, you might live through the night."

"What do you want Hoorne for?" I asked. Hell, there wasn't any point in playing dumb with this guy.

"He is wanted. It is not our job to ask questions.

Nor yours. Now where is he?''

''He's got himself a room south of here. I don't know where.'' The guy hit me again, not as hard, and I said quickly, ''Look, that's the truth. I know how to reach him by phone, but I don't know the address. We thought it would be safer that way.'' I was still trying to figure out who they were. There was a good chance they were part of the Chicom outfit, and if they were, we wanted them to find Steen. On the other hand, they weren't supposed to know that, so I had to make a good show of keeping it all a dark secret as long as I could. The way that guy threw punches, that wouldn't be too long.

''You will be calling that number soon,'' Frank told me. ''First, how did you come here from Seattle? And who helped you escape our people there?''

''Your people? I don't know who you mean,'' I said. It was the wrong thing to say, he hit me again.

''You know very well who I mean,'' he growled. ''I do not like this, Carl. I think we will take Mr. Crane with us, where he can be convinced that it would be better to telephone Dr. Hoorne. We will also want to know any warning signals they have for the telephone, and who he is working for. Now, once again, Mr. Crane, will you cooperate with us, or must we give you another demonstration? How did you escape our men in Seattle?'' He gave me another kidney punch, hard enough to stagger me. Things were getting a little fuzzy.

''If you mean those two guys in the Pontiac, we shot them,'' I gasped. ''They came driving up behind us in a big Pontiac, waving a gun, and we outshot them. That's all.''

''And you came to Los Angeles how?''

''We drove. In my other car, they'd shot holes in the one I was driving. Look, what do you want with us? We offered to sell you anything you want, why are you doing this?'' It wasn't hard to fake panic in my voice. I felt enough of it.

"You are selling us nothing," Frank said. "Gather Mr. Crane's things, Carl. He is checking out." Carl started to the bathroom to get my gear. There was a little alcove just short of the bathroom itself that had a closet with the suitcase in it.

"What is that on the bureau? Who does it belong to?" Frank asked.

I turned to face him, trying to estimate my chances. They looked about nil. He stood there with that knife, a big one about five inches long, waving it slowly in front of him like he'd enjoy using it. His face had no expression, just a cold look in his gray eyes. My gun was in his belt where I'd never reach it alive, and he knew it, but he wouldn't kill me if I made a dive for it. He knew so much more than I did he could disable me with no trouble at all. To keep my hands from shaking too much, I got my pipe out of my breast pocket. "OK, I'll answer your questions. Can I smoke?" When he nodded I took the butane lighter out of my pocket and puffed at the pipe. The stale tobacco was awful, but I choked it in.

"This stuff belongs to my girlfriend. We went out last night, and she wanted to make up before we got there. Left the junk here. It's just pancake and hairspray, see. . . ."

I picked up the can of hairspray to show him. Carl was still in the bathroom and it looked like my only chance. I flicked the lighter on and held it to my pipe for a second, then brought it down and held it in front of the spray can, pushed the button on the stuff. A sheet of flame a good four feet long shot out. The label had been right, the stuff was flammable as hell. I played the flame across Frank's face, watching his hair and eyebrows singe off, holding it in his eyes as long as I could.

He screamed, dropped the knife and held his hands to his face. "Carl!" he shouted.

As he did, I dived for the Luger, grabbed it from his belt and ducked down behind the bed. There was a satisfying click as I thumbed off the safety. Frank was stumbling around, but he wasn't as hurt as he thought he was. That stuff didn't make too hot a flame, and he'd closed his eyes before I got aimed at them. He was reaching for his own gun, and I thought it was about time to get the hell out of there.

The open glass doors to the balcony were behind me, and I turned and used one hand to vault over the iron railing, landing heavily on the gravel roof but still on my feet. I ran along the roof, getting a couple of startled looks from people in their rooms, until I reached the edge. I got the Luger into my belt and lay on the roof, put both hands on it, and dropped over the side, hanging by my fingers for a moment before I let go. It wasn't more than about a seven-foot drop from my feet to the concrete below and I took it lightly, going all the way down with the fall before bounding up. Some character was standing there watching me when I stood.

"That looks like fun," he said. "I think I'll try it." He tried to focus his eyes on me, but it wasn't easy. "Don't that look like fun, Mary Lee?" I saw a wide-eyed girl behind him.

"It's not what it's cracked up to be," I told him. "You ought to try it from the fourth-floor fire escape. Man, that's really fun." I left them standing there and walked quickly off toward the beach, certain that Carl and Frank were watching me from the room and hoping they wouldn't risk a shot. My back felt better when I turned a corner and got out of their sight. Just as I did, someone moved next to me.

"Mr. Crane," he said.

I jerked the Luger from my belt and damn near shot Sam de la Torres dead.

•   •   •

A couple of minutes later he had been filled in on
the events in my room, but he had to ask a lot of
questions to get the story. I was still shaking, and
fished around in my pockets but there wasn't anything to smoke. My pipe was lying on the bureau in
the Royal Inn. De la Torres offered me a cigarette.

"Thanks," I said. "Pall Malls. Isn't that disloyal
to the chief? I thought everybody had to smoke
Camels."

"That is better. Make some more jokes, so that
you can be ready to help plan what we must do
now."

I hadn't thought I was that obvious about being
scared, and I got hold of myself. So I'd had a close
one, you don't go around shaking until somebody
tells you how good for you it is to make a joke. I
mean, I'm not all hung up on masculine pride or
anything, but still. . . . "Sure, let's plan. How in hell
did they find me?"

"They must have followed the Vallery boy. They
did not follow you, I am certain of that, not until you
had the meeting. After that they may have followed
you, you went very fast and not too cleverly so that I
lost you as soon as you left that park. Remember,
you were warned that I would not be very close, I
could not tell if Vallery had someone else watching
besides the girl."

"So that's how they were able to follow me."

"Yes. They simply took a risk that I did not take
and moved in close to you. You saw nothing going
back?"

"I might have." I remembered the feeling I'd had,
that somebody might be back there. "I thought it
was you."

"You were not very careful. Still, it is as well for us
that this happened."

"Well for us? What good comes of all this?" I demanded.

"I know who they are. From your description, from the technique. They can only be Carl Heider, an East German, and a man who calls himself Frank Sobel although that is certainly not his real name. Sobel is a Russian, and they work for the security unit of the Communist Party of Southern California."

"CP? The real thing? Moscow people?"

"Yes. Interesting, isn't it? Moscow does not want Peking to have any secrets of missile interception. Our intelligence people give long odds that Russia and China will be at war in ten years. Both here and in Seattle, then, they were instructed to take Dr. Hoorne alive if possible, but failing that to kill him or use any means to keep him from the Chinese."

"OK. We know who they are, now what do we do?"

"We must report to our superiors, as they are undoubtedly doing now. I have a plan, but I must have approval from Mr. Shearing. Then, we will remove your things, take you to a safe place, and have a conference about what we must do. We must work very quickly, however. Did you set a new meeting with Vallery?"

"Yeah, I meet him at that park tomorrow at three. He won't have to find either Janie or me again. But if they were working in closer than you, they might have overheard us. Vallery was so sure we were alone in that park he wasn't very careful. I didn't hear anything, but who knows?"

"Yes. *Quièn sabe?* Besides, with modern electronics they could have heard you from a long distance if they had the equipment. Sobel is very good with electronics. It is because of that possibility as much as anything else that I want to discuss this with Mr. Shearing. This has gone far enough, we cannot let those people interfere now that we are so close to what we want." He led the way back toward the lighted streets, to a little bar with a telephone booth. We paused outside for a moment.

"What do you mean, we can't let them interfere again? I'm for it, but what do you have in mind?"

"I mean that it is time that we closed the books on Sobel and his people," Sam answered slowly. "They have interfered far too often as it is."

"Close the books? How do you do that? We can't go to the police, the FBI would be interested in why I was down here, at the least they'd have me watched and get in our way."

"I know." There was no emotion in his peasant face. In the half light it reminded me unpleasantly of Frank Sobel. They'd both had round flat faces, and both had that intense look in their eyes, the total professional absorption in their work whatever it required. "We take the only way we have, is that not obvious?"

"Not to me," I said, but it was.

He sighed. "We kill them, Señor Crane. What else should we do with them?"

11

SHEARING PACED NERVOUSLY in the narrow room, not watching where he was going but instinctively avoiding the ragged holes in the carpet that might trip him. We were in the wooden frame building that Steen was hidden in, with its peeling wallpaper and antique bathroom fixtures. De la Torres assured us that this was an absolutely safe house, everyone in it was reliable and no one in the community paid any attention to anyone else. Minding your own business was a strong ethic down here, as it is in most slums.

"You're sure you got Crane out without anyone being curious about him?" Shearing asked.

"Yes, sir. I watched very carefully. They had gone, taking with them only sufficient objects to be sure of fingerprints."

"They'll have Janie's too," I told him. "There was some of her stuff there and they took a bottle of pancake makeup I know of."

"That is another reason for approving my plan," de la Torres reminded him. "What other way have we?"

"Goddam it, I can't order murders just like that," Shearing protested. "It takes the Director himself to approve a termination with extreme prejudice, and he only goes for it when the subject's in our own organization."

"That is not always strictly true," de la Torres observed. "I know this is serious, señor, but if we do not remove these people they will jeopardize the whole plan. Must the Director know everything we do here?"

"If we act on our own and anything happens, you get disowned. You know that. I can't even be close to it, and you take the rap, right up to the big one, in the courts."

Sam nodded. "I know. It is a very important mission, and this is our only chance to carry it out. I repeat, what other way have we?"

Shearing stopped pacing and looked significantly at me, probably wishing I was somewhere else. "Run through what you have in mind." He sat in a dirty overstuffed chair, picking idly at the loose white junk popped out of a hole in the right arm.

It was Sam's turn to get up and pace, and he did. "What would be more natural than that Paul should call his girl and tell her of his narrow escape?" he asked. "And she will, of course, report this to her colleagues in Information Associates. She will also tell them where she is to meet Crane tonight. He will want to have her comfort, and she will go to him. They will choose a dark and lonely place, and we will do the rest."

"And you're counting on somebody in IA to pass it on to the Russians," Shearing said. "It might work. If they don't, we haven't lost anything."

"We can throw Dr. Hoorne in for bait," the fourth man in the room said. He was a big guy, about six three, with a big intelligent head and a lot of gray hair although he wasn't much over forty. He'd been introduced as Nick, a man who worked for de la Torres, and you didn't have to ask what his specialty was. He looked the type to go into a bar and challenge all comers, gray hair or not.

"No he can't," Shearing answered. "IA might send somebody themselves."

"Why should they?" Nick asked. "They didn't try anything in Seattle, did they? Anyway, we don't have to have Hoorne go, just say they'll meet him. Make the CP think they can find him. Damn it, chief, that outfit has killed off three of our men, not to mention two doubles we turned in their organization. It's time we took William Jordan and his boys out for good."

"He won't be at any kidnapping," Shearing said.

"He won't have to be." Nick laughed, a hard single syllable. "We know where to find him all right. And they won't be able to move without his approval. We set this up, Sobel and the goon troops show up, and while Sam takes them out I go find Jordan. He'll have to send his bodyguard after Hoorne and Crane and he'll be waiting for the report. I can catch him alone, might even take him alive, think what that'd be worth."

"Jordan?" I said. "You mean that professor guy who's always making speeches?"

"Yeah. You know him?" Shearing asked. He stopped picking at the holes in the chair.

"He's been at the University of Washington sometimes. I saw him in a debate with somebody, one of the conservative people. You say Jordan's in charge of security for the CP?"

"Yeah," Nick answered. "As tough and mean as they come. Fools you with that shortsighted apologetic look he puts on in public."

"He fooled me." I thought about this. Planning murders was a bit out of my line, but then it didn't seem real. "Do you have to kill him too? Once you remove Carl and Frank, isn't that enough? I mean, they've got it coming, but. . . ."

"But hell!" Nick pounded his fist on the rickety

table, knocking over Shearing's coffee cup. "People like that Sobel aren't too common, I grant you, but Jordon's up so high he can give orders to Russians like Sobel. You think about that one for a while, Crane. Here's an American giving orders to a captain in the Russian security organization. If we got him, it'll take a week to put somebody out here who can approve liquidations. By that time you'll be finished with your job. We need him out to protect you, Crane. Sobel they can replace tomorrow, but not Jordan."

"But—what proof do you have that he's . . . ?" I let it trail off. They were all looking at me, and they didn't like what they saw.

"What kind of proof do you want?" Shearing asked very carefully. "Something to take to court? I'll never have the kind of proof. I'd have to expose all my agents; then they declare a mistrial because somebody threw rocks at the judge. My people get themselves killed in 'accidents.' Finally we get a conviction, only the Russians pick up an American tourist, ram him through their courts, convict him, and offer to trade for whoever we finally put away. If we can get a conviction at all. Meanwhile he's been out on bail the whole time. We just aren't geared to fight these people by our rules."

"Yes, but—oh, hell, I suppose you're sure of him."

Shearing nodded. "No question about Professor William Jordan. None at all. But I still have the problem of the trouble this could cause. . . ."

"That's the guy that sent Sobel after you," Nick put in. "He could send somebody else tomorrow."

"None of us have real choices," Sam murmured. "Only imaginary ones."

I remembered Sobel's cold eyes and the way he handled the little knife. "What do you want me to do?"

"You make that call," Nick growled. "Tell Janie you'll call her back, you want to see her but you're still afraid and you have to be sure you're loose. Sound plenty scared in case her phone's bugged. Tell her to stand by, you want to meet her tonight, and give her the code so she knows she's supposed to pass it on."

"All right. Where's the phone?" Nick pointed to the adjoining room and I went in to make the call. We made it short, with me playing the part of a well-scared jerk. I got back to hear de la Torres and Shearing at it again.

"What the hell, you really want those outsiders in on it?" Shearing was saying.

"They are not outsiders. Sobel has kidnapped three of their people who were never seen again. They have lost their homes, their families to the communists. How can you call them outsiders, señor? Besides, if anything goes wrong, they will take the blame without speaking, and you will never have to make explanations to the Director."

"This gets more complicated all the time." He took out cigarettes, made a production out of tamping one down before lighting it. "I suppose it wouldn't hurt to have some help, they'll send everything they can get now that Crane's killed two of their troops in Seattle and scorched their Russian tough boy." He chuckled. "You're getting a hell of a reputation, Paul. You've probably got Sobel so mad he's run out of Marxist curses. OK, Sam, call your friends. I suppose you can get them this time of night?"

"I am sure, señor. They are always available when there is serious work to be done." He went to the telephone while Shearing poured coffee for all of us. In a few minutes we heard rapid-fire Spanish from the other room, a long pause, more Spanish, and finally "Bueno!" De la Torres came back grinning.

"Commandante Rubiro is delighted to assist us, and he will have at least ten men. That is many more than we have, and allows us to send someone with Nick to find Professor Jordon."

Shearing nodded, took a long pull on his cigarette. He leaned back, thoughtfully blew a smoke ring, and reached a decision. "OK. They're good auxiliaries. Let them handle the whole thing. You go coordinate and keep the rest of our troops out of there." He shook his head slowly, spoke more to himself than us. "I still wonder. If the Bureau's planted a man on them, we've bought the farm."

"A Bureau spy in the midst of the militant Cubanos?" de la Torres asked. "That is, pardon me, that is laughable. To do so he would have to have gone to Cuba before Fidel, gained their confidence at that time, gone to exile with them . . . not even the communists are that clever. Certainly not the Bureau. Major Rubiro is no fool, he will not allow anyone but his most trusted men on this mission."

"God help us, anyway. Nick, have you got Jordon located?"

"Yeah. I know where he'll wait for the reports." He stood heavily, nodding in satisfaction. "Sam and I have waited a long time for this chance. Don't worry about it chief, so L.A.P.D. has a disappearance or two, it won't hurt them none. Probably blame it all on some right-wing fascist outfit, and the Bureau'll get a new appropriation to infiltrate the Klan." He stomped out of the room muttering.

Shearing laughed without much humor. "It always irritates him that the Bureau puts so much energy into getting the right wing that it hasn't enough time for the communists. Not to mention the Mafia. Well, we'll make the Bureau's work easier after tonight." He looked up at me and suddenly looked away as if he didn't want me to see his face.

• • •

I sat in the passenger seat of Janie's VW watching the coast highway slip past. Off to our left was the beach, but you couldn't see the water because the highway was lined with beach houses all jammed together so there wasn't any yard between them. I wondered why they did it this way out at Malibu when Santa Monica with just as good a beach had some space between buildings. Out here the beach was private, and California has a law letting the public use any beach it can find; maybe they jammed the houses together to keep the peasants from getting down to the water.

I'd never been part of a deliberate murder. I tried to think of it as something else. A battle, an execution, elimination, even use the Cosa Nostra slang and call it a hit, but the word murder kept coming to mind. I couldn't give it my whole attention, though. We'd been followed from Janie's hotel.

"Are they still back there?" she asked.

"Yeah. One car, anyway. I hope they bought that story about us meeting Steen, I'd hate to have them try something too soon." It was easier to think about the mechanics of the problem than the end result, although the mechanics were none of my business. I was in this purely and simply because I knew about it, I wasn't kidding myself. I could ruin Shearing by telling the story, but if I was a part of it he could be sure I wouldn't. "You sure this canyon we're going to makes sense as a meeting place?"

"I think so," she answered. "I don't know much more about Los Angeles than you do, but the canyon areas are pretty wild, just where a man might hide out from the police. The Cubans have been hiding there for years."

"Who'd you report to in the Information outfit?"

"Prufro. He was the only one at the number

they'd left. I asked to speak with Dick or Bev, but he said they wouldn't be available for the rest of the night."

"Then we've solved the leak problem, haven't we?" I looked back at the car behind us. "He must have passed it on to the CP as soon as you hung up."

We turned off the highway onto an asphalt road. It ran inland a few hundred yards, then began to twist up the side of some steep hills, part of the Santa Monica Mountains. The canyon road ran along about halfway up the hills, thick woods above and below us. The edge of the road was guarded by a metal barricade set on posts, and beyond it was a drop of at least a hundred feet, sometimes more.

"I've been thinking about that. Prufro's the likely one, but he might have talked to someone else," Janie said. "We're coming to the place. Hang on." Fifty yards farther on she turned off the road onto a dirt track that wound up into the woods. It took a couple of curves and we were out of sight of the road. Behind us the car that had been following purred on past our turnoff. Janie backed up to the blacktop, headed us back to the beach area a couple of miles away.

"Hope you didn't lose them," I said. "Can't see anything back there. If they're with us, they're driving without lights."

"If that loses them, we couldn't have worked this anyway. We can't make it too easy."

"Right. Besides, they're supposed to know where we're going, aren't they? Wonder if they sent some people out ahead?" A quarter of a mile back toward the beach there was another dirt track, and we pulled off onto it, followed it steeply up the side of the hills, winding through the trees. "This must be hell in the rainy season," I said. "How would you get groceries up here?"

Janie didn't answer, being too busy trying to keep

the car moving in the deep ruts. We rounded another turn, and the headlights showed a small white frame house painted over with mystic symbols and grotesque figures, a typical artist's hideaway. We pulled alongside a collapsing garage, and got out of the car quickly and walked around behind the house to wait.

You could just hear traffic noises from the canyon road below us, and a couple of cars wound their way along it slowly, headed away from the beach. A stupid bird who didn't know it was dark trilled out a song. "Quiet as hell," I whispered to Janie.

"Shh." She took my hand and we stood there, wondering what would happen next. We waited another couple of minutes, then the silence was shattered by a single shot. A couple of others rattled off, then a burst that was hard to count. Everything was quiet again.

"Well, something happened," I whispered. I took the Luger out of my belt and cocked it, thinking that it hadn't done me much real good in L.A., but it was comforting to have. Nothing happened below for a long time, and I got nervous, wondering what had gone wrong with Shearing's ambush. We might have trouble getting back out of there.

The back door of the frame house rattled slightly, and I pointed the gun in that general direction, although it didn't figure that anybody trying to sneak up on me would make that much noise. I kept listening behind me, too, just in case he was making noise for a distraction. I may not be too well trained at the counterspy bit, but I can get around in the woods, and I hear pretty good.

"Señor Crane?" a voice called. I didn't answer, and the door opened. Sam de la Torres shined a light on his face, snapped it off and walked away from the house. "All is well," he said softly.

"Good." I moved slightly so that he could see where I was. If he was as nervous as I was he might shoot first and worry later. I know I was in a mood like that. "How many did you bag?"

"Six." He strode easily over to us, his caution gone now. "Three down on the road just now, and three more who came here earlier looking for Dr. Hoorne. They thought they were very clever, these city men." He gave a wicked laugh. "Commandante Rubiro has experienced jungle warfare experts in his command. It was hardly an equal contest."

"That is correct, mi amigos," a voice said behind us. I hadn't heard a thing, and from the way de la Torres jumped he hadn't either. A short little guy, much smaller than Janie, came out of the shadows behind us chuckling softly. "Who are your friends, Samuel?"

"Permit me to introduce you. Major Rubiro, I have the honor to present Señor Paul Crane and Señorita Youngs. Señor Crane, el commandante Jesus Maria Emmanuel Rubiro y Castro."

"At your service," Rubiro said. "Shall we go inside? It is not comfortable out here." When Sam protested, Rubiro added. "It is safe. If anyone comes you will be warned. Besides, for the moment the road is blocked, it will be clear soon." He led us into the house, which was quite comfortably furnished in contrast to the decaying exterior. The rugs were worn but good quality, and everything was hospital clean. We went through the kitchen to a large room in the front of the house. The walls were paneled in oiled mahogany, with built-in cases. The joiner work on the cabinets along the other wall was perfect, but everything seemed to have been built in, handmade, not bought in a furniture store.

"Please be seated," Rubiro said pleasantly. "Brandy? Some sherry, perhaps, señorita? We are well stocked here. It is a pity we will have to abandon these quarters now, but it has been well worth it."

Outside it had been difficult to see his features, but

when I looked at Rubiro in the light he had already put on a pair of dark glasses that covered the upper half of his face. "You are Major Rubiro?" I asked. "In what army?"

"My rank was given to me in the armed forces of the Republic of Cuba," he answered sadly. "But that was long ago. Please, what may I bring you?" Sam and I settled on brandy and Janie had sherry. Rubiro got them from a well-stocked bar built in to one corner of the room, then came to sit with us near the fireplace. It was a very pleasant room.

"You'll have to leave this now?" I asked.

"I am afraid so. It was an excellent place for our work tonight, I could be sure of nowhere else on such short notice, but there is a chance that the communists will have made a report of this location. I assure you it has been worth it." His smile was as deadly as a coral snake. "I thank you, Samuel de la Torres. You have given us enjoyable work tonight."

"Gracias. But we had nothing to do with it, of course. I could wish that you had not taken that so literally, I would have liked to see the men who came earlier. How long can you keep them missing before they are found?"

Rubiro shrugged. "Forever, if that suits your purpose. The channel is deep, and we have boats. Would you prefer it that way?"

"Yes." De la Torres sipped his brandy for a second, leaned back in enjoyment. Then a sour look came to his face. "We did not intend that you meet our friends here."

Rubiro nodded, flashed white teeth in his olive features. "But I had a strong desire to see the young people who were so important that your office finally gives us permission to do what should have been done long ago. I will not risk being insulted by asking what their mission is."

"You put that well," Sam laughed. "I can tell you

this, do not entertain the idea of trying to follow up this night's work. You could get in the way of something important. You will not meet these people again."

"That is unfortunate. They have said little, but of course they would be charming company. . . ." He examined us again with blank eyes hidden by the dark glasses. He was definitely a little man, no more than five and a half feet, quite slender, but when we'd shaken hands he'd almost taken off a finger without trying. He was wearing a dapper little military mustache, and his smile showed clean bright teeth, but these weren't the things you noticed about him. There wasn't anything really physical to notice, but the man gave off an air of danger that was more deadly than anything I'd ever experienced with Shearing's people. When he mentioned communists the smile was still there, but with it came a curl to the lips that made me think of medieval torture chambers.

"Sam tells me you took three of them down by the road and three up here. Are they all dead?" I asked.

Rubiro shrugged. "In a manner of speaking. Certainly they will not survive the experience." I saw Janie shudder slightly, then take out a cigarette and concentrate on lighting it. "You would not really care for the details, Señor Crane. To your way of thinking I am a barbarian. A useful barbarian, however."

I didn't know what to say. He'd about read my thoughts. "You were in Batista's army?" I asked.

Rubiro's smile got broader. "Yes. That, of course answers all questions about me and my men, does it not? You have learned your history of Cuba from the American news magazines, and it would never occur to you that some of those accounts might be mistaken, or even deliberate lies. All officers of Batista's army were without honor, torturers of women and

children, devoid of courage and interested in nothing
but power. As you are sure of that, I see no point in
continuing the conversation.''

"Well—OK, so I learned everything I know about
Cuba before Castro from the U.S. press. What was it
really like? The torture chambers were there, we saw
pictures of them. . . .''

"Yes. You ask what was it like? What is it like anywhere that the communists wish to take over? Assas-
sinations, murders, torture of prisoners, kidnapping
of the wives of soldiers . . . but all your papers could
find was the corruption of the government. I give you
the corruptions, Señor Crane. There was much of it,
although how much was ours and how much im-
ported by your gangsters who owned the casinos in
Havana would be worth discussing. But with all our
corruption, which seems to fascinate the American
journalists, do you seriously believe that my people
would not willingly trade Fidel and his murderers for
a return of the casinos and prostitutes?'' He looked
at his watch. "But we have no more time. My people
have taken the prisoners and the dead away from
here, and it is safe for you to leave. My best regards
to your superiors, Samuel. Tell them that I wait in
future to do their work for them, when they find
nerve to do what must be done. Hasta la vista, mi
amigos. And go with God. For those as soft as you,
He is your only protection.''

We left him standing in the paneled room, his
brandy held carefully between his hands. On the wall
behind him was a big Cuban flag and some pictures
of his graduation from military school.

12

DE LA TORRES stayed to confer with Rubiro's troops, and we drove on since we weren't supposed to be seen by them. After meeting Rubiro, I wasn't worried about anyone he trusted giving us away, but there was no point in spreading our identities around all the same.

The drive was clear, and we turned off the canyon road, headed for the beach. "Simple enough," I muttered. "I keep telling myself it's war."

"It is war," Janie said. "You'd better change rule-books, Paul. At least you can meet people now without having to worry about getting killed afterwards. I'd think you'd be glad."

"I am." I was thinking about Jordan. He'd seemed to be such a harmless little guy with his stories of government harassment which I'd thought paranoid. I got out my pipe and began to worry the gunk out of the bottom. Up ahead of us a car was coming, and I watched it warily. Then I looked back and saw another car behind pulling up on us. It reminded me of the road outside Carnation, and I watched it closely. The oncoming car went past, throwing light into the one behind us, illuminating the passenger's face for a second.

"Get off this road!" I shouted. "That's Sobel back there!"

I don't know what training they put Janie through, but it must have been good as anything the army does to drill its troops. She didn't say a word, just slammed on the accelerator to get around the next corner. "There's no turnoff here," she said after we'd made it. "Are you sure enough to risk going over the side?"

On one side of us was the steep hill they'd carved the road from. On the other was a drop of maybe thirty feet with trees and rocks in the part we could see, not very inviting, but it was a cinch we couldn't outrun whatever Sobel was in, not in a VW.

"We've got to get away before he catches up to us," I told her. "You figure out what to do, you're driving." I got the Luger out and checked it, wishing Janie was in my seat and I was driving. Maybe she could shoot as well as Steen. I knew I couldn't.

"There's a dirt patch ahead," Janie said. "Hold on, I'm turning off, it's kind of sharp." She braked hard and aimed the VW off to the right, up the hill. There was a wide dirt stretch that might have been the beginning of a driveway and might have been shoulder. The VW skidded on loose gravel and I saw a mailbox, so it was a road. She threw the shift down, gunning it to drift the turn, handling it almost as well as I could have, and we were bouncing up a rutted trail that made the drive to the Cuban stronghold look like a freeway. The VW lurched, fighting her for control, while we lost speed. The car behind slowed nicely, took the curve gingerly and came on after us. There wasn't any question now; before it might have been my imagination, but that guy was chasing us. We took another corner, this time under control.

"Stop this thing and get out fast!" I told her. I'd forgotten about that training of hers and she almost put me through the windshield. We were both out and running into the thick scrub brush and trees before the other car came in sight.

"Get down and don't move," I whispered. "Just stay right there."

She nodded and lifted her skirt, showing a lot of leg as well as the holster strapped to the inside of her thigh. The view of her leg was good, but I was more interested in the little chief's special she brought up. She held it like she knew how to use it.

Something jingled in my pocket, and I took out everything in it, coins, lighter, pocket knife, the works, and dropped it on the ground, moved quickly off the path we'd beaten into the bushes, moving carefully so as not to make noise. I might not be any jungle warfare expert, and I might have missed Rubiro moving up behind me after the fight, but I do get out in the woods to stalk deer. I wondered if comrade Sobel and whoever had been driving him did. I also wondered just how good his eyes were after his experience earlier. He could obviously see well enough to be out hunting for me tonight.

There wasn't a sound, but I had time. I just hoped Janie could keep still long enough to make something happen. Out of the canyons there had been a little moon, about a quarter full with some low clouds, but in here everything was shadowed. After a minute or two I could see dimly, bushes and trees and chapparal, with high weeds in between everything bigger. It wasn't easy country to move in quietly, and from the silence Sobel's people were standing still, hoping to hear us crashing around running from them.

I waited a couple of minutes longer, carefully choosing a route. They couldn't be close to me or I'd have heard them, and shooting in that light was likely to be pretty haphazard. It was time to stir something up, and I did by making a dash off to the right, angling back a bit toward the road but still going uphill. That located me for them, and when I was quiet again I heard them moving, one of them staying on the road, the other trying to be quiet as he punched through the chapparal. If the one on the road wasn't trusted in the weeds, he had to be very bad, because his partner was making enough noise to cover a regiment.

I waited until the guy on the road had got up ahead of me and moved off on his own. Actually, he was the better of the two, it was hard to hear him coming. Before they had me boxed I was going to have to do something. By now I had time to think about it, this wasn't just a night exercise from basic training or a deer stalk. That didn't seem to be too encouraging a thing to think about. I concentrated on the problem, ignoring the danger and planning what to do. I was plenty scared, but if I let it get the better of me that would be the end.

What advantages did I have? Sobel probably didn't have too high an opinion of me. He'd seen me plenty scared when he'd caught me before, and there wasn't any reason for him to believe I was going to be very difficult. He'd been careless with the hairspray bit, but I hadn't shot him or anything like that. I could hope he'd take me for a lightweight and that he'd be mad enough to make a mistake. From the noise, they were no match for me in the woods.

I moved carefully toward the guy crashing around in the bushes, letting his movements cover any sound I was making. That lost track of the other one, but he was farther away, and I could only deal with one at a time. When I got close enough to the noisy one, I stamped on a pile of weeds and ran across his path, shouting "Help!" and anything else I could think of to make me sound hysterical.

He took the bait, started running after me. I took a long dive into the weeds, rolled over and lay still, waiting for him, but hoping he wouldn't get there.

My trail led him past where Janie was hiding, that was one reason I had shouted, so she'd know it was me. The guy ran right by her. He couldn't have been more than five feet from her when she shot him.

That little .38 made all the noise in the world. You could hear echoes of it all over the canyon, and somewhere up above us on the dirt road a dog started to bark. I angled down toward the road, taking plenty of time to make as little noise as I could, and got to where I could see the cars there, took a comfortable position close to them and waited some more. There was only one man out there now, and although he'd have Janie located from the shot, if she stayed still she could hear him coming from a long way off. He really wasn't very good in those weeds, and neither one of them had any business going in there after us.

The dog was still barking up on the hill, but I didn't see any lights. Whoever lived up there wasn't coming down to investigate. Maybe he thought it was a backfire from the road below, or a firecracker, or maybe he just liked to mind his own business. Or, of course, maybe he was calling the police. I was hoping that possibility would occur to the other man out in the woods before too long.

He was all right on the road. I didn't hear him coming, and I almost didn't see him. He got up to his car and crouched there, listening, maybe hoping to jump in and get the hell out of there before anything else went wrong with his mission. I had to give him full credit, he was a persistent son of a bitch. Six of his troops taken out by the Cubanos, another one shot down out there in the woods, and he was still there. I'd have been long gone by now. He was waiting for one of us to be careless, because he stayed by the car, not moving, listening hard.

I took careful aim, started to take up the slack in the trigger, and held it. I couldn't shoot the guy like that, and I knew it. I tried to talk myself into it. It looked like Sobel, although in the dark it was hard to tell. I told myself this was the character who pounded in my kidneys, stuck a knife in my ribs. He was all set to do me in. In a fair fight he could take me apart. He'd got out of his medium there in the woods and gave me an advantage, and now I had him. All I had to do was pull the trigger. It was no use, I couldn't just shoot him down. That's the real difference between the professionals and the amateurs. It's not so much skill as attitude. If you're ready to take all your advantages instantly, you don't need so many.

I heard Janie move out in the brush. She was probably wondering what happened to me, and it had been a long time to just sit there listening, probably looking at the body of the other guy. For all her training, she couldn't stay still all night. My target tensed, but he held his pose.

It was a long minute while I wrestled with it, trying to convince myself that I had to shoot. Finally I said, "Drop it and don't move. No, don't try to stand, just let go of the gun."

He didn't move. If he'd tried to run, or point the gun at me, I'd have been able to shoot him, but he didn't do anything. "Let go of the damn gun, Sobel!" I shouted. "I can shoot you five times before you find out where I am." He still didn't move, trying to locate me from my voice. It wouldn't have done him a lot of good, since I was lying down behind a tree with not much showing, but maybe he was a hell of a pistol shot. I thought of aiming for his gun arm, but that was ridiculous. Even in good light I couldn't be sure of shooting that well.

I heard Janie out in the weeds moving slowly toward us. The situation was getting a little silly. The last thing I needed was for her to give him something to shoot at. "Stay out there, he's still armed," I called softly. "Now, for the last time, will you drop that damn gun or do I have to shoot?" But of course

I knew the answer. I mean, about all you can do with a gun is shoot it, isn't it? He started a dive, moving suddenly, trying to roll under the car, and I fired three times. The Luger made a flat crack, nothing like as noisy as Janie's .38 had been, and when the echoes died away the damn dog was barking again up on the hill.

13

NOTHING HAPPENED FOR five minutes by my watch.
There wasn't any sound but the dog, and he gave up
after a while. I stood cautiously, keeping my pistol
ready, but I didn't think there'd be any need for it.

"Janie?" I called.

"I'm all right."

"Good. Let's keep the noise down." I walked up
to where she was, almost stumbling over the body of
the first man. He was lying face down in the weeds
and seemed to be sort of shrunk up, although that
was ridiculous. There was plenty of blood. When
Janie got to him I took a deep breath. "I suppose we
ought to get his papers," I said. "The Agency will
want to know who he is."

She nodded and I rolled the guy over. I'd seen him
before. "It's Carl something or other," I told her.
"Sam says he's East German."

"But—" She was staring at the body. "That may
be his name, but I knew him as Bert Facks. One of
Vallery's people." She was breathing pretty hard,
and I knew just how she felt. It made me feel better
to know it was getting to her too.

"Get back to the car," I told her. "I'll get his

papers." She nodded and went off, not too steady, while I thought about something else and went through him, collecting everything I could.

She was sitting in the VW when I got back to the road, and I had to do the same thing for Frank Sobel. Then I went back to my tree and hunted around until I found the empty cartridge cases from my Luger, collected them, and got in the VW. She let me drive, and I got the car backed around Sobel's Chevy, turned left and followed the canyon away from the beach, out toward the valley freeways. We climbed through the hills, passing the driveway to the Cuban place, not seeing any other cars. Janie didn't say a word.

"Pretty good shooting," I said. "One shot in the dark, at a running target. You're pretty good with that thing."

She nodded, got out another cigarette. Even in the reddish flame of her lighter she looked pale. "He would have had you if I hadn't. . . . That was my first one, you know. I wonder if you get used to it?"

"I don't know. Dr. Prufro didn't say anything about telling him. . . . He must have, of course. If cleanup squad out there before morning. What do you make of Facks being there?"

"I don't know. Dr. Prufo didn't say anything about telling him. . . . He must have, of course. If Sam knew him as a CP security man down here, he had to be the plant in Information Associates. No wonder they had leaks in that organization."

"Yeah. Well, we plugged that one. They took quite a chance sending him with Sobel to get me, they were pretty confident that I'd never be able to identify him later." We didn't say anything else, drove along the freeway. After a few minutes I put my arm around her, but she couldn't move very close in the bucket seats and the road twisted too much to let me drive that way. We went back into our private worlds without touching. I found a closed gas station and stopped at the phone booth, dialed the number I'd been given.

"Night deliveries, can I help you?"

"Larry." We went through some identification stuff. "Is the chief there?"

"Yes." It took a couple of minutes, then I heard Shearing's flat electronic voice. "Go ahead. You got a problem?"

"Two of them. Both dead. We left them with their Chevy on a deserted dirt driveway about a mile south of the ambush site. I figured you'd want to get somebody out there to clean up before morning. They can't be seen from the road, but we heard a dog bark up on top of the hill, somebody must live up there. The name on the mailbox is Weatherby."

"Couldn't you think of a better place . . . no, I guess you couldn't. You've done well, if the cops have to pick up somebody with a load of dead bodies, right now I'd rather it wasn't you. Tell me about it."

I ran through it from where we'd left the Cubano hideout, giving him the details of where his troops could find the bodies. He whistled when I identified Carl as Bert Facks, but otherwise didn't react at all. It seemed unreal, like something that had happened to somebody else, and I was worrying about his reference to the police. It had been self-defense, but that would be hard to prove now that I had their papers.

"OK. Hang on a moment, I want to see if we can use the same disposal squad as the other operation." He was off the line awhile, came back on. "OK, we've got somebody working on it. Now, how well did you clean up out there? Leave anything behind?"

"No. I found the brass from my gun. I suppose somebody could get casts of the tire tracks if they had anything to compare them to, but I don't see how we can be traced. I'm pretty sure we weren't seen."

"Good. Look, I'm sorry this happened. We should have known those two weren't caught in the earlier action, but that's the trouble with cooperative deals, you lose control at critical moments. You'll be glad to know Nick's part of the operation was satisfactory. He has a hole in his shoulder but he took his man. We shouldn't have any more trouble from that quarter for a while, it will take them at least a week to get in a replacement with authority to order removals." There was a long silence punctuated by the sound of a cigarette lighter. "You sure you didn't leave anything up there?"

"No," I said disgusted. "I'm sure I did. When we first got out of the car I took all the rattly junk out of my pockets and dropped it in the weeds so I could move around without anybody hearing me. There's a pocket knife, a butane lighter, and some loose coins up there." I patted my pockets. "I did think to keep my wallet anyway."

"That lighter of yours has your initials on it," Shearing said.

"Yeah, I know. Want me to go back and get it?"

"Hell, no," he said emphatically. "That's all I need, to have you caught wandering around in the bushes with a couple of stiffs. What chance would you have of finding it in the dark anyway?"

"Well, it won't be too far from Carl's body. I emptied my junk near Janie's stand, and she got him. . . . If you looked with a light you might spot it."

Shearing let out a long sigh, something more expressive than words. "I don't suppose Janie left her calling card, or a sweater? You didn't drop anything else?"

"Not that I know of." I turned to her. "Boss wants to know if you left anything back in the hills?" She shook her head. "She says no. So they've got my lighter, what can anybody make of that?''

"You might be surprised what the L.A. sheriff's department can make of anything. Especially if they get a tip from the CP. If it gets out that one of their people is dead, and your initials were on a lighter near the body, it won't inspire trust. OK, we'll just have to see that the disappearance is kept mysterious, and I'll have the troops look for your junk, although I doubt they'll find it. With no bodies out there, it's not evidence of anything. Get back to the safe house and stay out of sight until the meeting tomorrow. Take Janie with you. I don't want her questioned, and she isn't needed at the Hollywood Roosevelt. This time tomorrow we might have this whole thing finished.''

"Let's hope so. How do I play it with IA tomorrow?''

"Like nothing happened tonight. You took your girl out, you spent the night together, and you didn't see a thing. Let the CP stew over what happened to their agents, it ought to give them a real headache. Not that we're likely to be bothered with their people for a while after the job we did tonight.'' He sounded pleased with himself. "Their whole goon squad's down the drain, that's one less factor to worry about in this operation. All right, I know where to find you if I've got anything.''

I turned to Janie. "He says we go to the safe house. Both of us. The Cubans are supposed to clean up.'' We piled into the VW for the long drive back to Santa Monica and Venice. I thought there might be something behind us, and I took enough turns to lose anything but the Batmobile, and I'd have given that trouble. When we pulled into the alley behind the Venice house, it was nearly dawn.

My last-minute briefing was from de la Torres in an upper-story room of that decaying house. I sat in a folding chair using my pocket knife to clean my pipe. The Cubans had found it and the change, but not my lighter. Since it was left near the knife, that was something to worry about, but there wasn't a damn thing we could do.

"We will have Dr. Hoorne available at any moment after you meet them," Sam was saying. "If the money is at all satisfactory, make any arrangement consistent with your cover story. They may want to take you and the money together with Dr. Hoorne, and that is not reasonable given the character you have presented to them. You will want the money, and he will go with them."

"Isn't that kind of dangerous for Steen?" I asked.

"I'll survive," Steen answered. "Hell, you've had all the fun this trip so far, give me a chance, will you?"

"You're slipping, Iron Man," I grinned. "You don't sound much like a watery-eyed electron counter anymore. Just what are you, old college chum?"

"That is none of your business," Sam answered for him. "You have good reason to know he is an expert in his field of physics, and that is enough. This whole mission has been designed to get Dr. Hoorne and the Chinese buyers together, and your speculations are not needed, Señor Crane."

"Yeah." I swallowed the reprimand, but he couldn't keep me from remembering that Steen could shoot holes in the driver of a pursuing car with an unfamiliar weapon, and hold the tiller through a gale. "Once I've got the money, what then?"

"Try to stay alive and bring it back here without being followed." Sam eyes me closely. "You are aware that you have asked for a large amount from their secret funds, and they will not willingly give it up. Furthermore, you cannot rely on any protection from us. The primary mission cannot be sacrificed for rescues."

I nodded, thinking I should have realized it before. It was a little late to back out now. "I can insist on reasonable precautions and procedures from them, of course."

"Naturally. You are not known to them as a fool, quite the opposite. Do nothing foolish now."

"Thanks. I won't. OK, I get the dough and come back here. Then what?"

De la Torres shrugged. "Mr. Shearing takes the money, you are paid for your work, and you have your boat here. . . . A long vacation in the islands will do you a world of good."

"And I never do learn what all this is about?"

"Do you really want to know?" He was serious about the question, and I found on reflection that I probably didn't. I was curious, because something seemed a little odd about this whole deal, but knowing answers like that could be unhealthy.

I glanced at my watch. "About time to start for that little park." I checked the loads in my pistol, tucked it in my belt and arranged the loose shirt over it.

"What do you see in that little gun, anyway?" Steen asked. "It's too big to conceal properly, the caliber's weird, the barrel's too light for accurate shooting. . . . You ought to carry a good .38."

I grinned. "Thanks. I notice you got some good use out of it. I like it. It's as accurate as I am, and I'm used to it. Any more sage advice, O man of laser beams?"

"Nope. Good luck, skipper."

"Thanks, Iron Man. You may need it more than I do."

14

I WALKED TO the park. Venice was swarming with people of all shapes and sizes, old Italians and Jews living on retirement in houses they'd bought when they were the only people here, or clustered in former resort hotels converted to homes for the aged, anterooms for the funeral homes that sprouted like ghouls. There were Mexicans who couldn't speak English at all, and the hairy shapeless wonders of both sexes. Artists and musicians crowded the bars. A couple of young girls in floppy outfits strolled barefoot on the sidewalks, shouting with glee when a mail truck pulled over and one of the longhairs burst out. They sat together on a low cinder wall by the street and one of the girls put on the mail carrier's sweater complete with the pony express rider official patch. It was warm and nice and beautiful, and I had no right to think that the taxpayers were paying him to deliver the mail and could arrange their own truth and beauty.

There were blocks of houses separated by sidewalks with no street between rows and houses at all. One block was all in the typical rundown condition, peace symbols and garish colors splashed everywhere, except for one house which had been put back in new condition. An old man sat on its porch staring off into space, not looking at the squalor he now lived in, dreaming with the pride which had driven him to keep his house in order.

I got to the bench very early, but Bev was already there. She sat staring with the same expression as the old man I'd just seen. I noticed that for all that was bothering her she'd put on a spectacular outfit, a dark green playsuit and gold sandals, her hair combed back and tied with the inevitable scarf.

"Hi, kid. Lost your last friend?" I asked her.

She turned with a start, shook the cobwebs out of her brain. "Do I have one to lose? Sit down, Paul, let's talk about this."

"Oh, Lord, another wasted meeting. You don't have the money, right?"

"We have it. Dick's waiting not far from here with—with one of their expendable people. We're supposed to go there, you see they have the money, and get Dr. Hoorne."

"What happens after that?"

"I don't know," she stammered. "They give you the money and Dr. Hoorne goes with them to talk to their technical people."

"OK, let's get on with it. Remember, a nice safe neutral place for the meeting. I'm not following you to any lonely spots."

"It will be all right." She made no move to get up, turned to me desperately. "Have you thought about my offer? I could get twenty thousand dollars if you wait until I see some things. Just come with me and tell them Dr. Hoorne has changed his mind, he's found another buyer. Do that for me, Paul, please, I'll—I'll be nice to you, you'll see, we could. . . ."

I cut her off. "Why?"

"Because I'm scared. You should be too. All we've done so far is give them some silly documents nobody's looking for, but your friend knows something important, it says so in the papers. . . . I didn't know what I was getting into, and now it's too late to stop it unless you help. For God's sakes, what can I do? I'll promise you anything, just stop it before it goes any further.''

"Can't do it, Bev. We've got to have that money. Steen's wanted, we need it to get him somewhere safe. Your twenty grand just isn't enough, you know that. And you can stop offering me your body, I won't take another man's girl.''

"But—oh, all right, they're not far. Please be careful, Paul, they—This is the last one, if I can get Jim through this we're going to, to. . . .'' She stopped talking, stared over my shoulder. I turned to see what she was looking at.

Dr. Prufro was running across the park, his suit coat unbuttoned and flapping wildly, his vest undone. There was grease on his hands, and he'd got a little smeared on his forehead which was dripping with sweat.

"Beverly, Beverly, thank God I got here in time, I had a flat, I thought I'd miss you. . . . Beverly, don't go with him! Don't do anything with him, don't even talk to him, he's a government agent, he and that Youngs girl, they're both agents!''

When I realized what he was saying I tried to shut him up, but he ignored me. "Beverly, you should have left a way for me to call you, I've been trying to reach you all day. This man, last night, this man and the Youngs girl, they killed some people, and then he said he'd have to go through their pockets so the Agency would know who they were. He's a government spy, they're just trying to get evidence on you.'' He fumbled in his pockets, breathing hard, and came up with something I recognized. "Look, here's his lighter. He killed Bert Facks.''

She stared at him, then at me, back to him, not really understanding what he was saying. I looked at my watch. We had a few minutes to go before three, we could still make the meeting.

"Look, kid, what's with this creep? The last time I saw him was in Seattle when he paid me for some documents I gave him. Now why in hell would a U.S. agent give top secret information to him?"

"As evidence," he gasped. He looked in a bad way, he must have run a long way to get there and I thought he might have a heart attack. "I know how you people work, you want to catch the leaders," he panted. "But it didn't work, you've got me but you don't really have anything on Beverly, nothing you can charge her with, she'll be safe."

"Oh, cut it out," I told him, but it was no use. I could see that she believed him.

"They've got enough evidence on Jim and me both," she said. There was a toneless resignation in her voice. "It's too late, Doctor Prufro. Thanks for trying, anyway." She stood there staring, but he turned on me and shook his fist. I thought he was going to fight me, his face was white with rage.

I thought fast, came to a decision. "Look, you're right. I do work for the government, and you're both in big trouble. We can put Jim Vallery in the electric chair with what we have on him. But we aren't interested in small fry like you, we want your contact. We want the Chinese agent you deal with, and I'll trade you Jim Vallery's life for him."

"What—what do you mean?" There was a little life back in her eyes, a little hope again. I had to talk fast to keep it from going out.

"Take me to the meeting and act natural. We go through with it just as we were supposed to. If it works and we get the Chinese agent I'll arrange to have all three of you forgotten. That's the deal, Bev. You, Prufro, and Vallery are out of it if we get the mysterious Chinaman. Otherwise—do you think Jim can hide forever? I've already got the two of you. By the way, you're under arrest." It sounded good, anyway.

"I—Arthur, what do you think? Can he make a deal like that?"

Prufro shook his head sadly. "I don't know. I thought Jim had kept you out of this. Does he really have evidence against you?"

She nodded. "I was with Jim when we paid him for some documents, and when we arranged this meeting. And Jim actually gave them the money. Oh God, can they really hang him?" she asked me.

"Depends on what state they convict him in. Some federal prisons use an electric chair. I think they still hang at McNeil Island in Washington if you prefer that."

"You do not have to be deliberately crude," Prufro whined. "You are frightening Beverly."

"Damn right I'm frightening her," I snapped. "And you might try being a little scared yourself. You've ruined an important operation, don't think we won't make it as tough on you as we can. I've made my offer, now take it or leave it, time's running out."

"You promise Beverly complete immunity?" Prufro asked. He mopped his face as I nodded. "Your word as—you are an officer, aren't you?"

Hell, I thought. What difference would it make? But he was that kind of character. I didn't have the authority to make the deal, but I could say I could. "Of course. My word as an officer of the government. We'll let all three of you go. . . . You'll have to tell your whole story, everything you know, of course."

"All right, Beverly. If you take him to this meeting with the full knowledge of the government, they can't prosecute you for it. I think you should."

"But I can't—I—I'll give something away, I know I will. . . ."

"For God's sake, if you want to save your boyfriend get hold of yourself," I growled. I thought I was doing pretty well as the tough-guy act. I tried not to think of what Shearing would say about the way we'd muffed this. "Come on, let's go to your car."

She turned away quickly, starting to lead me off. I stopped her. "OK, Prufro, come on. I can't let you wander around loose."

"But he's not supposed to be at the meeting," she protested.

"He won't be. I've got a place to stash him. Come on, let's get moving."

We climbed into her big Caprice and I directed her around corners, through a couple of alleys, looking back to be sure we weren't followed, but I didn't think we would be. We'd eliminated the people who liked to follow me. I turned them into an alleyway, then into the garage to the safe house.

Steen came into the garage with a pistol. "For God's sake, what's this?" he said. "You got the money already?"

"No time to explain. Haven't made the meet yet, got to go before we miss it. Keep Prufro on ice. He knows I'm a government agent, says he hasn't told anyone else. He knows about Janie, no others in our operation, keep them out of his sight if they don't want him to. He was obviously in the car with Sobel and the other guy last night. Go on, get out, Prufro, you've come to rest. Tell Dr. Hoorne everything you know, it'll be good practice for the next time."

He nodded, then buttoned his vest and smoothed his hair before he got out of the car. "I—I hope it will be all right, Beverly," he said. "I—good luck to Jim, too." He walked out with Steen, very slowly, a wave of saddened dignity.

"OK, kid, on to the meeting," I told her. "Move, Bev! If we're late the deal's off."

"All right." She backed out of the garage. "I— Paul, please, do you mean it? Will it be all right, will you let us go?"

"Sure, kid. No problem." None at all, I thought. Provided that Harry Shearing was in a mood to approve my deals. I wasn't sure how he'd take this, and we had only minutes.

They'd picked a good place. Santa Monica has a big amusement pier, and we met on the beach under it. Plenty of people milled around, and nobody paid us any attention. Crowds were strolling along the beach, grabbing hot dogs and eating them while walking. A group of leather-jacketed tough kids shot pool and drank beer in a place down the beach, while a girl no more than fifteen stood outside, gyrating to hard acid rock, her eyes closed. I began to wish they'd let her go inside. Above us we heard the organ music of a carousel, a gay happy tune.

Beverly walked down to the sand like a man on his way to a hanging. She was obviously scared, but she'd been scared of the whole deal before, maybe they wouldn't see her any different. She'd been all right in Seattle, but after that she'd been nervous; maybe it was the newspaper pictures of the two characters in the Pontiac, there's nothing like a couple of dead bodies to bring the realities home to you.

Vallery was waiting with a man who might have had some Oriental blood in him, but he could as easily have been an American with Indian ancestors. He was wearing dark shades and a thin nylon jacket over his sports shirt, and there was something about him that reminded me of Major Rubiro. The sunglasses, of course, but there was more, that aura of danger and death that the Cuban had. He lounged against a piling with his hands in the windbreaker

pockets and didn't say anything when Vallery introduced him as Mr. Hudson. We didn't shake hands.

"Anything phony?" Vallery asked.

Beverly gasped, looked at him, looked away, and
said, "No. He says he can bring Hoorne when he sees
the money." She looked defiantly at Hudson and
Vallery and I took in a deep breath. "I still don't like
this, but you're safe. Nobody followed us."

"Good." Vallery held out a big folding-type briefcase. "It's in here. You can't take it out and count it
because of the meeting place you wanted."

"Sure. I'll manage." I squatted on my heels and
opened the case, fished around in it. It was full of
money. "How much is here?"

"A hundred thousand dollars. That's all they had
in cash, I can't do better." He seemed worried.

"And your cut?"

"I—I already have mine, if this works out. That's
your share."

"You guys haggle good, don't you? This take it or
leave it?"

"Yes. There won't be any more."

"I take it. Give me a few minutes, I'll have Dr.
Hoorne here."

"Just a minute. Bev, go with him and see that he
doesn't do anything funny."

"But. . . ."

"Go," Vallery ordered. There was an edge to his
voice I'd never heard him use with her before.

"All right." She went over and kissed him. I stood
close to them, too close for her to pass the message
that she'd intended.

"Let's go, then," I told her. "Come on, kid."

She tore herself away from him and followed me
down the arcade. We went up hill to Ocean, and
along it to a delicatessan.

"You try warning him again and the deal's off," I
told her. "I can't trust you out of my sight, can I?"

"I—I won't tell him. I just wanted to. . . ."

"Yeah. You're not a very good actress anyway. Everybody on that beach thought you were scared of something." I dialed the number of the safe house.

"Yes?"

I went through the identification drill. "That last routine's compromised, the Henderson girl is with me," I added. "Steen, they're at the foot of the Santa Monica pier. I'll meet you at Ocean and Colorado. Right now."

"All right, I'm on my way. Here's somebody."

"Yeah." I didn't really want to talk to him, but what could I do? "Yes, sir."

"You are being overheard by the girl?" Shearing asked.

"Right."

"I have the story from Dr. Prufro. There was nothing else for you to do under the circumstances. We can discuss why it was necessary at another time. For now, can you keep the girl from giving them a warning?"

"I'm going to try like hell. I thought I'd suggest that I keep her while they have Steen." I heard Bev gasp as she realized what I'd said.

"I like that," Shearing replied. "Of course they might not buy it. Can she keep all this a secret?"

"No sir, not a chance. Given any time alone with Vallery she'll spill it all."

"Paul, this is extremely serious." It sure was, he'd used my real name over the telephone after warning me about it. "You must take whatever action is required to complete this mission. There is to be a meeting of the National Intelligence Board tomorrow and this operation is the agenda. Do you understand the significance of that?"

"Not really."

"It is extremely significant." There was a long

pause. "I have no other instructions. I know you'll do your best."

"Sure. I always do. Is the deal I made OK? You approve?"

"What else can I do?"

"Then tell her that. With whatever restrictions you intend to make." I turned to Bev, still holding the phone so that Shearing could hear too. "This is my boss. He's going to talk about the arrangement we have. Here." I gave her the instrument. She listened for a minute, and I thought I saw some improvement in her expression. Then she handed it back.

"You better get going," Shearing said. "I told her I'd confirm the deal provided she continues to work with you. Satisfactory?"

"Yes, sir." I put the phone back on its hook and led Bev out.

"He—seems like a very nice man. It is going to be all right, isn't it?" she asked hopefully.

I'd never heard Shearing described as nice, and it certainly wasn't a word I would use for him, but hell, if it made her feel better it was all right with me.

It didn't take Steen long to get to Colorado and Ocean, and we walked down under the pier in near silence. Vallery and his escort were waiting as if they'd never moved. Vallery looked at Bev and raised his eyebrows, she nodded and muttered something about everything being all right. He licked his lips and handed me the briefcase. "You're to wait here until we're gone, Crane."

I bent over and looked through the case. The money was all there as far as I could tell. They hadn't done anything clever like substituting cut-up newspapers. I stood, nodded approval. "OK. But I won't be waiting alone, Dick."

"What—what do you mean?" I'd got the escort's attention too.

"I mean you're taking my friend with you. I've got nothing you want now. I want a little security for Steen, thank you, and your girlfriend will do nicely. She stays with me."

"No." Vallery was emphatic. "We'll be gone several days."

"I've got lots of time. You believe in freedom, right? Good business principles, right? She isn't going to get raped, but by God I'll have security for my buddy." I shrugged. "So it can take several days, I expected that. Just so he comes back."

"What—what will you do if he doesn't?" Bev asked.

"You won't like it," I told her. "But there's no chance of that, right? Your boyfriend is a good business man, right? You're not leaving with both of them, Dick."

"I think he has a good idea," Steen added. "I think, now, that I will not go unless she stays with him."

"No," Vallery insisted. "It—no, I'm not leaving her alone with you for that long."

"It's all right," Bev said. "Don't you trust me? Jealous?" Scared as she was, she wanted to hear him say it.

She didn't get the chance. Before Vallery could answer, Hudson intervened. "She will stay here. We will argue no more, come with us, Dr. Hoorne."

"All right," Steen answered. He looked around nervously. "If we are not back in—how long, Dick?"

"No more than two days," Hudson answered. "He will be here by this time of the day after tomorrow." The voice was even, a rich cultured voice with an educated quality as if he'd had professional speech training. "Now, let's go."

Vallery started to protest again, but Hudson cut him off with a quick precise gesture. Bev and I stood there, watching as Steen and Jim Vallery walked slowly up the hill, stood there long after they were out of sight. Behind us the carousel played a happy tune. Each of us wondered when we'd see our friend again.

15

I DON'T THINK she blinked her eyes the whole time she could see Vallery. After they were out of sight I waited a couple more minutes, then walked her to her car. I took a long twisting route, ending up five blocks from the safe house. We parked and I led her through the alleys and across lots until I was sure we weren't followed, finally into the safe house. Janie let us in.

"How did it go?" she asked. She was stern, all business, and I wondered if Shearing had read her out for getting caught. It seemed reasonable, and my turn was coming.

"OK. They took Hoorne and went off into the toolies. What next?"

"In there," she said. She pointed to a door. "I'll take Miss Henderson. Beverly, we can go upstairs if you'd like. Do you want anything? Coffee, a drink?"

"No. Just to get this nightmare over with—no, nothing thank you, Janie." She'd been staring at Janie, trying to convince herself of something. "Can you tell me what's going to happen now?"

"Sure. Let's go talk." Janie led her out, and I went through the door she'd indicated. Shearing had set up a command post inside. There was a big table in the middle of the room, which might have been the old dining room of the house. An enormous map of the Los Angeles area was spread out on the table, covered by a piece of plexiglass, and Nick was standing there with a pair of earphones and a plastic hush-phone mike. He was moving little colored blocks of wood around on the map with one hand. His right sleeve was empty, and I could see bandages across his shoulder. Sam de la Torres was hunched up in a corner of the room with another set of phones and had a little switchboard and microphone boom on a table in front of him.

Shearing was under the window in the big over-stuffed chair that must have been brought in from the other room for him. It still had holes in the arms, but he wasn't playing with the stuffing at the moment.

I looked at him sheepishly. "What can I say?"

"You can begin by explaining how you overlooked a third man in the pursuing car. Suppose it had been one of their enforcers instead of Dr. Prufro?"

"Hell, there was a lot happening out there, Mr. Shearing." He'd once invited me to call him Harry, but I hardly ever did, and this didn't seem to be the time for it anyway. "He must have got out of the car and stayed hidden, not moved at all. When we bailed out of the VW we were trying to stay alive, not see who was chasing us, you know."

"Miscounting the number of men hunting you is not the best way to stay alive. As it happens, you are correct. Prufro tells us that he was forced to accompany Bert Facks, as he knew him, because Facks was getting worried about you, and wondered how many sides Prufro was playing on."

"So he was their leak, after all."

"Yes. The CP has been blackmailing Dr. Prufro for a long time. To avoid helping them, he contrived to get himself fired from Sandia Corporation. Or so he says, we haven't bought all of his story yet. It was through Prufro that Facks entered the Information Associates organization.''

While he talked, Shearing kept an eye on the map table. I saw that the red block, which seemed to be Steen and his escorts because the others were black with numbers on them, was driving around in the Pacific Palisades, up and down streets in a random pattern. The other cars were in a box about a mile on a side around it.

"Wasn't that kind of nutty?" I asked. "I mean, why would a CP agent pose as a free-lance information buyer?"

"Apparently there are people in this country who will sell information to a clean-cut young man like Vallery when their scruples prevent them from dealing with the communists. But that wasn't Facks' primary mission. He was after the same thing we are.''

That one whizzed right past me and I said so. The reading out seemed to be postponed, but I was pretty sure it would begin when there was more time. I pulled a folding chair away from the wall and sat where I could see Shearing and watch the map board. If they weren't going to chase me out, I was interested in what happened next. I got my pipe out, still thinking about Shearing's last statement. "They were looking for the Chinese agent?" I asked. "Wouldn't they know who he was?"

"No more than we do. The Chinese have no love for the Russians. I don't suppose there is anyone they do think of as friends at the moment. In any event they aren't going to trust one of their top people to an ideologically unreliable ally like Moscow. This agent is quite special to them, he really is an anti-missile scientist. You've already seen the lengths the CP will go to prevent Peking from getting that kind of information. Facks wanted to find the Chinese contact, probably to eliminate him."

"And the poor old geezer was being blackmailed."

Shearing nodded. "Hardly surprising. The vast majority of people who work for the communists do so out of fear. Many of them convince themselves they are doing the right thing, of course. People do have a tendency to try to justify their actions to themselves. But Moscow has never been very enthusiastic about employing someone they don't have a more tangible hold on. Presumably the Chinese will use the same technique since most of their people once worked in cooperation with the CP net."

"What happens to Prufro now?"

"We can place him on a college faculty somewhere and get him a grant to do classified research. The CP will find him and try to use him again, and we'll run him as a double agent." Shearing took out the Camels, lit one, blew a smoke ring. "He may not last very long at that, but then again he might. He has some experience trying to keep Vallery unsuspicious."

"Hard on him, isn't it?"

"What do you want us to do with him? He nearly got you killed three different times, are you really concerned about him?"

"No. Not really." I suppose I wasn't. I didn't like the pompous old man—he wasn't really all that old, but he acted like an old man—but there was something a little pathetic about him. Well, I suppose it beat going to prison or worse, which was what he deserved. "What about Vallery and Henderson?"

"That will depend on the outcome of this operation. In any event we will want to know all about their buyers and sellers for the Bureau. After that I may have another use for them. . . . Sam, do they seem to have any fixed direction yet or are they still playing games with us?"

"Still moving about, señor. They will long since have assured themselves that they are not being followed visually, we must presume they are attempting to detect an electronic tracking device."

"Yeah. Better hold off pulsing that unit much."

"I have. That is why we cannot be sure where they are at this moment."

Shearing nodded in satisfaction, leaned back with his cigarette. There was a cup of cold coffee on the windowsill behind him and he drained it. "Let's just hope they don't take the simple method and strip Hoorne. Or if they do, maybe they won't throw his shoes away."

"You have a tracker in his shoe heel?" I asked. "Be easy enough to pry them off and see."

"Not the heels, in the soles of his sneakers," Shearing said. "And it isn't just a tracker, it's a transponder. Know how that works?"

I dredged up my electronics and thought for a second. "You've got a transmitter and a receiver, and it only transmits when it gets pulsed from the outside."

"Exactly. So the transmissions are very short, and we hope not likely to be detected by any sweep they may make. When all we could do was get an unarmed man sent to their agent, this seemed the best procedure. After all, we went through this whole charade so they wouldn't suspect our involvement. It ought to work."

"What if it doesn't?"

"We have alternate plans, but Steen is pretty much on his own." He looked at his watch. "I could wish they would knock off the games and get moving."

We waited another ten minutes, while Nick moved the red block only once. Then he nodded, moved it again, onto the Pacific Coast Highway, headed back for Santa Monica. After a few minutes it was obvious they'd taken the Santa Monica Freeway, headed east. Shearing's chase cars were all behind the red block.

"He's out of our net," de la Torres reported. "You said to keep the number of pulses down, and he came onto the freeway quickly."

"Yeah, that's all right. Call Clover Field and get the plane warmed up just in case."

Sam turned to his switchboard, plugged in to one of the jacks. He talked softly into his little mike so we couldn't hear the conversation.

"You've got an airplane?" I asked.

Shearing nodded. "Army loan, an experimental superquiet job. Couple of boats standing by, too. I've got every agent I can trust from the whole Southwest, and it isn't enough. We're spread thin like butter on a student newlywed's toast." He looked around for more coffee, found the pot was empty. "Sam, you better get over to the airport. . . ."

De la Torrres cursed in Spanish. I don't know much of the language, but when I took it in high school one thing I learned real good was how to cuss somebody out, and I recognized some of the more choice expressions. "There is no pilot," Sam reported. "I'm sorry, señor, but a civilian delivered the airplane and the army intelligence man who came with it cannot fly. He did not think to report it before, he thought we would send a pilot. We did not have a man at the airport; if the plane was needed I planned to go myself."

"God damn it," Shearing said. He said it slowly, almost reverently, as if he were inviting the Almighty to come in and personally conduct the missing pilot to hell. "These goddamn cooperative ventures never work. Nick, can you handle it?"

"No, sir." It was the first time the big man had spoken to us since I came in the room. "Not that ship, chief. It takes two hands to fly that beast. Just a second, sir." He listened attentively, moved the block of wood onto the San Diego Freeway headed north. "They're going out in the Valley now." He moved a chase car onto the Santa Monica several miles behind the red block and pointed the others toward the San Fernando Valley. "There's some traffic in Sepulveda Pass, we may catch up with him . . . oh, damn it!"

"What now?"

"Number three's been pulled over by the Highway Patrol."

"Using up another two or three minutes," Shearing said. He looked squarely at me. "You can fly, Crane, it's in your record."

"Depends on what the airplane is," I said nervously. "I don't like the sound of that experimental job."

"Sam, take him out to Santa Monica and get him in that plane. I want the two of you in the air. I'll take over your desk."

"Yes, sir." Sam looked at me impatiently.

"But I don't know if I can fly that. . . ."

"Get out there and find out," Shearing snapped. They were all looking at me.

"Yes, sir. All right, Sam, let's go."

16

IT WAS THE goofiest airplane I'd ever seen. They'd
started with a sailplane, one of the big Schweizer jobs
with about a sixty-foot wingspan, really an enormous
beast to carry only two passengers. I'd flown one a
couple of times, taking off by being towed behind a
jeep out in the eastern Washington deserts, but that
was a long time ago, back when I'd done other wild
things like race sports cars. Unpowered planes can be
fun, you get up and find a rising air current, keep
hunting others. The whole airplane doesn't weigh
much over a thousand pounds, and if you're lucky
and know where to look for thermals you can stay up
all day. They are, however, a sport for young and
foolish people, not a married man, or so I'd let Lois
convince me. I'd let my ex-wife convince me about a
lot of things, I was beginning to realize.

They'd added a motor to this sailplane. There
wasn't room forward of the pilot, so they'd put the
motor back behind the cockpit and run a shaft over
the pilot's head. The propeller was on a big strut
sticking up from the nose, and the damn thing looked
like a butter paddle, a big four-bladed job made out
of wood. I wondered where they'd found anyone

who still knew how to make a wooden variable-pitch propeller.

I looked the thing over, turned to Sam. "That? You've got to be kidding." But he didn't say anything, so I climbed into the cockpit. It seemed familiar enough except there was an extra lever over on the left, along with another handle that looked like a throttle. There were the standard controls for a Schweizer sailplane, plus a lot of instruments for the motor, and they were standard enough except for where they were placed. Little bakelite signs were riveted to the instrument board in unlikely places, giving normal instrument values and other information. Evidently a lot of people unfamiliar with it had to fly this plane. Right up at the top panel was a big notice: "AIRCRAFT LIMITATIONS. NEVER EXCEED 6000 RPM OR 114 KNOTS IAS. SOLO FROM FORWARD SEAT ONLY. INTENTIONAL SPINS PROHIBITED." Well, that figured. Anybody who'd spin a sailplane, even one with a motor, was crazy. Another notice told me that 10° YAW ABOVE 120 did something, but the last words had been cut off the notice plate to make room for a landing-light switch.

I picked up the checkout sheet hanging on a clipboard in front of me and read it off. It was pretty complete, and under it were some more sheets giving values for engine operation and a lot of instructions on how to fly the ship. Sam had already climbed into the rear seat, which was a snug fit. The bird hadn't started with much room to spare, and the addition of engine controls and various other gear cut into it severely. There were also several boxes fastened here and there including one long one that ran past me into the rear seat area.

I swiveled around. "Look, if I get this thing off the ground we're still likely to come down hard. Christ,

Sam, it isn't like getting into a strange car, you know.''

"Señor, if we must go back to Mr. Shearing and confess that due to my failure to check everything twice we have failed in this mission, I think I would rather crash in the airplane. If you cannot fly it, you cannot, but if there is any chance. . . .''

He looked so goddamn courageous there, and I wasn't forgetting back outside the Royal Inn he'd told me to make jokes so I'd feel better. . . . "OK, strap yourself in and we'll see. You got all your radio gear?''

"It is all installed.'' I looked over my shoulder to see he was right. In addition to the other junk he was wedged in with about a hundred pounds of electronics. I was glad he was a lightweight, this thing obviously wasn't designed to carry much payload.

I heaved around on the stick, looking out to see that the control surfaces did what I expected them to. Then I examined the strange handles, checked them off against the clipboard instructions, and yanked them around. As the clipboard said, we had dive brakes and spoilers, which I might have to use in landing. It even told how to bring her in on a short runway, which I thought was nice of them. The cockpit wasn't really all that different from sailplanes I'd flown, and this began to look more possible, although I'd never have tried it if de la Torres hadn't been so damn brave about it. I shoved the canopy open and started to climb out, and Sam shrugged. "You cannot do it?" he asked resignedly.

"Yeah I can do it. I can probably get us killed too, but I won't do that by running out of fuel. I'll have a look in the tanks, thank you.''

The gauges told me we had plenty of fuel, but I like to know things like that myself. It took a while to find them, they'd hidden the blasted intakes pretty carefully. I unscrewed the caps and stuck my finger down in the wing tanks, felt gasoline. As I did I remembered something I'd seen once and never forgot. Once in Seattle I happened to look out the window of a jet I was about to be flown away in to see the captain, a gray-haired four-striper, out squatting on the wing poking his finger in the fuel tank. If I'd got a picture of that I could have made a fortune putting out safety posters. I even made up a story about him. Somewhere, many years ago, he'd had a gauge stick on him the day the mechanics hadn't topped her up, and by God. . . .

I released the tiedown lines and got back in, still not convinced this bird would fly, but determined to make a stab at it. Presumably it had got to Santa Monica from somewhere else, it sure wasn't built there. As I climbed in it wasn't too comforting to note the big "EXPERIMENTAL" painted across the fuselage just under the name of the Burbank aerospace company who'd built the ship for the army.

I got settled in and called the tower for instructions. "This is Experimental N5 niner eleven, request clearance and runway for takeoff."

There was a long pause, then a crisp voice came on with the unemotional tone that all flight control people seem to have. "Experimental N5 niner eleven, you have priority." He started reading weather conditions and altimeter settings, and didn't seem concerned that there wasn't a flight plan on file for us. Shearing seemed to be able to get cooperation when he needed it.

The engine started easily and I was amazed, you could hardly hear it. It wasn't anywhere near as loud as a lawnmower, more like a good car with the muffler slightly worn even when I ran her up to the redline on the tach. I got taxi instructions and let the brakes off. There aren't any brakes and landing gear on Schweizer sailplanes, but somebody'd installed very standard Cessna spring retracting gear so that wasn't any problem. The beast taxied like a normal plane, except that with that big slow-turning wooden prop out front I had the crazy feeling we were floating sideways in a chopper. I can't fly a helicopter.

I ran the motor up to redline again at the head of the runway, compared all my figures to the checkout list. There wasn't anything to it. The dual ignition system worked fine, the fuel pumps poured the stuff in as advertised. I called for takeoff and got that priority signal again, released the brakes, and off we went. At sixty knots she lifted off by herself and we climbed easily at eighty.

She flew fine. In fact, she was fun, and I stopped thinking of her as a beast. This was a real ship, but weird, because you couldn't hear the engine at all, and there wasn't much sound from the air rushing past outside. The controls were hard to work, which wasn't surprising, the Schweizer isn't really designed for either the weight or the speed we had. The rudder was sloppy as hell, first having no effect at all and then over-reacting, and you didn't get to relax and enjoy the ride, but still—she flew, and it was so quiet I could imagine I was in a sailplane. It was a funny feeling, all that quiet power, floating around over a big city. We could have come down to a hundred feet over the beach and nobody would know we were there unless they happened to look up.

"I'm turning north and heading out toward the San Fernando Valley," I told de la Torres. "Better report to Shearing."

"I have just told him we are airborne," Sam said. "I did not want to speak to him until I was sure you could handle the craft."

"Yeah. I like confidence. Look, you're going to have to navigate, *amigo*, I don't know this area well at all." I had the chart in front of me, but I wasn't

confident that I could watch where I was going and
fly that weird ship at the same time.

"No sweat." He sounded relieved, which wasn't
too surprising. Then we hit a sharp updraft when we
passed over the Santa Monica mountains, and I had
to shove her around a little to get back in control.
She'd yaw like hell, and the nose pitched up with
right aileron. There were a couple of other surprises
too. When we were level again Sam continued as
if nothing had happened. "You may follow the freeway north for the moment." We flew on, and I
revved her up a bit more to about ninety knots indicated. Below us the San Diego Freeway wound
through Sepulveda Pass, with brown hills above it on
both sides. Off to our left about a million white gar-
bage trucks snaked up and down the hills to where
they were filling in a canyon with the waste from a
day's living in Los Angeles. I wondered how long it
would be before they had all the canyons filled, used
the dirt from the hills to bury the mess, and made a
nice flat topped mesa out of the steep hill country
down there.

De la Torres listened for a moment on his phones,
then passed a set to me. "This a different circuit
from your aircraft radio, if you will put this on. . . .
Let me know if you wish to speak to Mr. Shearing, I
can patch you in. Be careful what you say, this is not
a secure circuit."

"Yeah." I got his headset on, stuck on the ship's
headset on the other ear, making my head look like a
Mexican bandido with his ammunition belts crossed
across his chest. "OK, let's have the boss," I said. At
least we didn't need interphones in the ship to talk to
each other. It wasn't anywhere near as loud as a car
at seventy although we were going a lot faster than
that.

"You are connected. Go ahead."

"Chief? Larry here," I said. "Over."

"How's it going? Over."

"Fine. We'll probably crash any minute, but I've got her fooled into thinking I can handle her right now. What comes next, over?"

"Make the best possible speed in the direction you are headed until you have visual contact, then use judgement. Sam, you may tell him whatever you think he should know. Out."

We had crossed the Santa Monica Mountains now, and the smoggy mess of the San Fernando Valley was laid out in front of us. The first thing you saw was the blue squares and curves of about a million swimming pools. I had to bring us in pretty low to be sure of following the freeway in the smog, and wondered what the air traffic control boys would say about that. The hell with FAA regulations, I wasn't about to fly this thing without seeing the ground clearly. There were a lot of cars zipping along the freeway and I didn't see how we were going to pick the right one, but as long as Sam wasn't worried I wasn't going to start. "OK, what next?" I asked him.

"They are still on this freeway headed north, several miles in front of us. Try to close with them, when we approach I will identify the car for you. It would do you no good to hear the reports I am getting from our ground people, they are in code anyway."

"OK, but after we spot them, what happens?"

"You make absolutely certain they do not see us, and follow them. We chose this airplane because no one will hear us approach with it. We must not alarm them until they reach their destination, and not even then."

"That shouldn't be too hard, unless they go too far. From the papers I've got here, this thing uses about ten gallons an hour and we have a bit over forty gallons. We use more at the speed we're going," I added.

"I think they will stay somewhere in this area," Sam told me. "We think they intend to leave this country for Mexico very soon, and they would not want to go too far north. I am surprised they are going north at all, I had expected them to go toward Mexico." He pronounced it with an "x" like Americans do.

The San Fernando Valley stretched out on both sides of us, a bowl full of smog with houses at the bottom, a blaze of red tile roofs and blue swimming pools and garages and cars, prosperity U.S.A. There's never been a rich republic that would defend itself. Sooner or later they hire it done so they can enjoy their riches. I wondered if it was our turn now, because the soldiers always end up robbing the paymaster.

Down below the freeway was clogging up, the chase cars would have problems keeping up. When I asked, Sam told me they were well behind our man but wouldn't want to be close up anyway. They still had electronic contact.

The traffic thinned out when we got to the end of the valley and into some more hills. The smog vanished, and I climbed for altitude. The map showed some reasonably high mountains ahead of us, with the highway winding along in the passes. Some miles ahead the highway would get to its highest point, about 4,000 feet, at Tejon Pass. I tried to remember where I'd heard the name before, and it finally came to me. Fort Tejon was the place where the U.S. Army used to station the Camel Corps back in the days when Secretary of War Jefferson Davis wanted the camel to replace the horse for cavalrymen in the Mojave Desert. Prospectors claim there are still wild camels out in the Mojave, but they never bring any in so it's probably the rotgut they drink.

We passed over some small cities named Newhall

and Saugus, then on to more wild country and the Tejon Pass. I didn't want to risk getting low enough to see the car very often in that country, so we had to rely on whatever Sam was using from back there in his half of the cockpit. He seemed to know what he was doing. We were a good fifty miles north of Los Angeles, and there wasn't much of anyplace the people we were chasing could go. The Tehachapi Mountains and the San Gabriel Mountains run together at Tejon Pass, with nothing but the Mojave Desert to the east and the Sierra Madres to the west. I concentrated on flying the crazy ship and let Sam worry about tracking our quarry.

We'd been up a little short of two hours when we reached Tejon Pass. By then I'd throttled back to keep from passing the car below, and through the binoculars I'd had a look at it, a big dark blue car. When you get to Tejon the road starts down fast into the San Joaquin Valley, the big green kidney-shaped splash on your contour map of California. It looked about like that to us from the air, a big green and brown flat saucer ringed by mountains but stretching out beyond the horizon in front of us.

"If they're trying for Mexico they've got a hell of a strange way of getting there," I told Sam.

"It would seem that way. We have confidence in our sources, but perhaps we are wrong this time."

"Yeah. Right now they're a long way from anywhere."

"It seems clear that they have left the Los Angeles area. I will signal for Mr. Shearing and his command people to come north."

We cruised on into the San Joaquin Valley. Along the highway it was a maze of canals and green farms, but not far on either side it trailed off into brown sagebrush. The great earth scar of the new California aqueduct system designed to bring water for even more people to crowd into Los Angeles stretched out of sight to the northwest. I could see a lot of oil derricks over to our left.

The blue car was a couple of miles in front of us, traveling exactly 65 mph, which let us track it at 60 knots indicated air speed. There wasn't much wind so our ground speed was about the same, although I could only measure that from the map.

"Hey," I called. "They've turned off the freeway." I had a look at the map. "Let's see, west onto State Highway 166. That road doesn't go anywhere much. Off to the edge of the valley, about twenty miles. If they follow it past there they could make it to the coast, but there's fifty miles of pretty rugged mountains in the way."

"We will send some people up the coast road," Sam told me. "But it is a strange way to go to the coast, even to avoid being followed. They are very careful, but I cannot imagine they would do that." He looked around him. Below there was nothing, a few fields, some ranch houses miles apart, and not much else. "It is very lonely country here."

"It sure is." I flew on past the turnoff they'd taken, got a couple of miles farther and turned left to parallel the car. The road they were on was absolutely deserted. "If you guys want to try to follow them in cars, you've got your problems," I told Sam. "All they need is one spotter anywhere on that road, the traffic density is like nil. In fact, look over there a couple of miles from the freeway, there's a car parked there. They're slowing down. . . ."

I cut back the engine and let us drift over toward them while Sam got busy with the binoculars. Nobody would ever hear us out there, and he could probably see anyone take a close look at us. We were a silent ghost floating over the deserted farmlands.

"They have exchanged cars," Sam told me. "Now the car we were following is going back toward the freeway. . . . I saw three men enter the other automobile.''

"They aren't taking any chances, are they? Your electronics people are on the other side of the mountains, they won't be able to check . . . which one do we stick with?''

"The new one." He got the radio going again, with no luck, but he kept trying. In about five minutes someone answered, and Sam read off a string of numbers.

"What was that?" I asked.

"We have codes for most contingencies. It was not unexpected that they would take a new means of transportation, and I have described it. A brown Ford automobile going west at a high rate of speed with no new passengers so far as I can tell. I have asked them to remain interested in the blue car as well. Have you more to add to that report?''

"No. Pretty good code you've got.''

"We had a lot of time to think of the possibilities. Unfortunately, while I can make voice contact with our people, the range of the transponder is not sufficient to allow us to check.''

We flew on, over newly plowed farmlands, some vineyards, then into a series of low rolling hills, brown already this early in the spring, and beyond them a forest of oil derricks. There were all kinds of the things, big steel ones, the little pumps that look like a duck drinking water, even old wooden towers. If there was anybody out there to watch them I couldn't see him. There was almost no traffic on the road below, maybe one car every twenty minutes.

"They're stopping," Sam said. I was busy with the plane for a moment, found time to look ahead. The car rolled into a little lot by an isolated building at a crossroad.

"If anybody looks up, you tell me," I said. "Until they spot us the first time, we can risk getting pretty close. I'm going to get west of them so we're in the sun, it'll be almost impossible to see us anyway." We flew over our quarry at about five hundred feet and maybe that far away in horizontal distance. There was a filling station diagonally across from the building they'd stopped near, and nobody looked up at us. They wouldn't hear us. It was an eerie feeling, almost like being invisible.

"Only one man left the car," Sam said. He was watching with the binoculars. "It appears to be a store of some kind."

"Maybe they're getting beer for the desert trip," I suggested. "I'd like to have a cold beer myself." The wind blowing in through the little ventilators was hot and didn't cool us at all. Down there on the road it would be even worse. I went on a mile or so west of them, banked and circled over the hills, coming a little closer, then circling away again. We were at the very edge of the San Joaquin Valley. According to my map the town below us was Maricopa, and by the looks of it there weren't more than fifty or so houses in the whole town. In spite of all the oil fields around there weren't any swimming pools. The houses could use a coat of paint for that matter. But they had all outdoors for yards, and the sky was clear.

"He has come back out. You may be correct, he has a paper bag," Sam reported. He was quiet for a long minute. "That is an Oriental man. They have traded for someone who was in the car that met them, I think. There was no Oriental with them when they left Los Angeles."

"That's interesting . . . do you think they've traded anyone else? Like for instance Dr. Steen Hoorne, so that we're following the wrong car? Because if they did, we've lost them, Sam, and I don't think the boss is going to be very happy about it."

17

IT TOOK AN hour to get an answer to that question. Sam didn't have the gear to pulse Steen's electronic tennis shoes and none of the cars were in range. We had some negative information in less time. The blue car went up into Bakersfield with Vallery and a couple of other chaps aboard, but no Hoorne. Or at least, no tennis shoes belonging to Hoorne, and no sign of him from a quick visual check at ninety miles an hour. They didn't want to close with the car for a careful look.

The brown Ford we were chasing went on up State Highway 33, through a medium-sized town called Taft. A couple of teen-agers spotted us from below and stood on the sidewalks pointing up at us, but the Ford had already gone by. We followed it north into a low stretch of hills, a finger of the Temblor range that borders the west edge of the San Joaquin Valley, watched him until they came down through a one-store town called McKittrick, burning along the highway at about seventy. There wasn't much traffic on that lonely road, but what there was passed that Ford like it was standing still. People out there seem to think of a hundred as a nice cruising speed.

Just about ten miles north of McKittrick they turned left onto a blacktop road, and not long after turned left again onto a dirt track into the oil fields, went along that for another couple of miles, and stopped at a clump of sheet metal buildings out in the middle of nowhere. I didn't approach very close, circled far to the west to keep in the sun, and we watched them park the car in a shed and go into one of the buildings. We hadn't been close enough to make out any faces with the binoculars.

A half hour later, with us still circling over the hills west of them, a panel truck drove past on the highway and a few seconds later we got our answer. Steen's shoes, hopefully with Steen in them, were in the abandoned drillers' shacks.

"That's great," I told Sam. "Now what? I hate to point this out, but we're going to run out of gas if we stay up much longer. Can somebody take over the watch from the ground?"

"Possibly. Follow that panel truck until we are out of radio range from our target."

"Glad to." We cruised on up the road. Even at max speed the crazy plane didn't make enough noise to disturb the jackrabbits and coyotes we could see down on the desert. The country was completely empty, nothing but sagebrush and oil rigs, with a lot of space between oil rigs. When we got far enough away, Sam used his radio to call the truck.

They were the first of the caravan, the others were being routed differently so they wouldn't pass the oil camp, we were told. "The boss wants you to keep a check on them until we can get the rest of the troops in position," they added. I didn't recognize the voice. "Another half hour to an hour. And make a good terrain check."

"In an hour I'll be running on fumes," I told him. "Maybe I can find a thermal and play sailplane games, but we're too overloaded for it. Where do I bring it when I can't keep it up any longer?'' It would have been possible to land on the desert, but I wouldn't want to try it unless I had to. Schweizer sailplanes do it, but they don't have a thousand or so pounds of motor and other extraneous weight. The crazy plane had a low stall speed and glided beautifully, but still. . . .

''Map shows a field right up ahead at the next crossroads. Place called Blackwell's Corners. We'll get set for you to land there, OK?''

''OK. I guess.'' The idea of a field I'd never seen was a little more intriguing than the sagebrush, but not much. We cruised back, throttled way down, to float over the oil fields and hills. There wasn't a sign of movement at the enemy camp, but we didn't want to get too close. Sam kept looking at the derricks, finally spotted a guard who seemed to be mostly interested in watching the road a couple of miles east of him. After that I stayed even farther away.

They didn't have much of a camp. There were two sheds and the larger enclosed corrugated-metal building with windows they'd all gone in, plus three abandoned derrick towers. The dirt road leading to the place was graded wide and flat, straight as an arrow like all roads out here. There wasn't any point in making curves in them, you didn't have anything to go around, a road engineer's paradise. With nothing to watch it was as silly a way to waste half an hour as I've ever spent, and finally I cut it off, heading for the landing field before we really did get low on fuel.

It wasn't much of a field. Somebody had graded out a straight patch of desert, stuck up a worn old windsock, there was a ranch house with the roof caved in, and a couple of miles off in another direction was a colony of big house trailers, presumably for oil drillers who didn't like the delights of Taft or McKittrick. The panel truck, a car, and a big camper were parked at the end of the runway, our welcoming committee.

Whoever had laid out the field knew the prevailing winds. The runway, if the dirt patch without tumbleweeds on it could be called one, faced directly into what wind there was. It seemed to be long enough, and I've landed Schweizer sailplanes crosswinds on the sandbars along the Columbia River banks, so I couldn't really complain. Our bird weighed a lot more and wasn't as responsive, but I didn't think I'd have much trouble.

I took a long glide in across the highway, dropped quickly after we crossed the transmission lines somebody'd put in the approach path, and skimmed her along the runway until I thought I was a couple of feet over it. When everything felt right I pulled on the spoiler lever. Unfortunately the control was on my left and so was the throttle. I didn't have enough hands to give her more juice and compensate for the loss of lift, and we were about four feet off the ground instead of the foot or so I'd thought. We dropped like a rock, bounced off, hit again, yawing hard while I fought with that big barndoor rudder, overcompensated, and turned her sharp the other way.

"Hold on!" I shouted. I was still fighting with her, and somehow kept her upright although I wouldn't want to say how. We fishtailed dcwn the runway, losing speed, with me never quite getting back in control until we finally swung all the way around, a complete horizontal ground loop.

"We're down," I told Sam. I didn't really want to talk to anybody. I haven't made that sloppy a landing in ten years, and my ears were burning. At least we hadn't bent anything. "It's over."

"Thanks be to God," de la Torres muttered. He opened the canopy and looked around as if he didn't believe he was safe, and I realized he'd been scared

stiff the entire time we were in the air. When he got
down he gave me a silly little smile.

Shearing was waiting in the camper. Janie was
with him, and he told me they had Beverly Henderson in the panel truck with another guy I hadn't met,
although nobody explained what the hell the girls
were doing out there. Nick was still moving things
around on maps. The map spread out on the dinette
table of the camper was an auto club road map, and
there were a couple of gas company maps tossed over
to one side as if they'd examined them all and picked
this one as the best. None of them showed any terrain
features.

"You have a better map of this area?" Shearing
asked.

"There's the air navigation chart," I told him.
"It's got terrain and more roads than this one. Want
me to go get it?"

"Let Peters go after it. Manny, you want to go out
to the plane and find the chart?"

"Yes, sir." Peters was one I hadn't seen before, a
thin sort of guy who looked like he'd blend into any
crowd, and I couldn't remember anything outstand-
ing about him as soon as he was out of my sight,
which is probably the way he'd want it. In his business a memorably handsome profile would be a lia-
bility. After he went out there was room to stand by
Janie, but she was all business, concentrating on the
map, a one hundred per cent government agent.

"What in hell are they doing way out here?"
Shearing asked.

"We saw nothing to tell us," Sam answered. "It
appears that our information about their intentions is
incorrect."

"No." Shearing was definite. "The Henderson
girl told Janie the same thing. They intend to get out
of the country fast, possibly tonight. It was one
reason she didn't want to be separated from Vallery.

She was afraid they'd take him with them."

"No chance of that," Janie said. "Unless they start from Bakersfield. Does Paul know about that?"

"I know Vallery probably stayed in the other car, the original one," I said. "What's this about Bakersfield?"

"We lost them in that goddamn city," Nick answered. "We had to hang way back, there was only the one car to follow them with and no electronics to guide us, and we lost them." He cursed under his breath.

"Better to lose them than scare them off," Shearing commented. "But our immediate interest is this group out here. Show me on this map where they are."

I looked at it and shook my head. "Hard to do with any accuracy. It doesn't even show the blacktop road they turned off on, much less the dirt track they took after that. They're right in here, somewhere," I added, indicating a spot, "but I wouldn't want to stake much on exactly where." Peters came in with the air navigation chart, and I looked that over. The scale was better than the auto club map, and it did show hills and the blacktop road. "OK. Here's the little finger of the Temblors that comes down into the valley. . . . They're on the flatlands, just south of the tip of it. But this damn chart only shows one-thousand-foot contour lines and the ridge peters out gradually, it's not a cliff behind them as you might think from looking at this, although it is a steep hill."

Shearing studied it closely. "Any signs of roads in the hills behind them?"

"Yes, sir. You can see the blacktop road that goes past their camp angles off to the right here. Not far from where it turns there's a dirt and gravel track that climbs up into the hills and runs south along the ridge behind them, maybe a mile from them and oh, nearly a thousand feet above their level give or take a couple of hundred. It doesn't show on this chart.''

"But to get to that road you'd have to go past their camp?"

"From this end. I don't know where the other end connects. Maybe nowhere.''

"Could you get from that road to their camp without being seen?''

I thought about that one for a while. "A good woodsman might if he was careful. It's pretty rugged out there, chaparral and greasewood, and it gets steep in places. It wouldn't be easy.''

Shearing eyed his cigarette as if he'd got a taste of something bad. "I see. Well, you're one of our experts on the wide-open spaces. Sam and Nick have some experience creeping around through the weeds, but the rest of my people are strictly city boys.''

"You have been known to work in some very rough country,'' Sam reminded him.

"Thanks. But I'm due to catch an airplane out of Bakersfield in about an hour. Washington wants me.'' Shearing grimaced. "No choice. I'm supposed to brief the National Intelligence Board about this operation first thing in the morning. I tried to point out to the deputy director that we hadn't finished it, but. . . .'' He lit a fresh cigarette while we all looked at him. "I could hardly tell them that my senior people are incompetent and the mission will fail if I'm not actually present, could I? Sam, you're in charge, let's see what we can make of this before I go.''

"Yes, sir. As Paul says, they are in an old oil driller's barracks some three miles from the highway, two from this unused blacktop road. The country around them is very flat, a man on one of those derrick towers could see for miles. Behind them is a finger of the hills as you see on the map, and within a quarter mile the country is very rough. They are in a splendid place, it will be very hard to get close to them."

"And you definitely saw an Oriental in the car. Did you recognize him?"

"I have been trying to think, señor. I believe it was Bruce Ching, but it is hard to be sure. He walked like a young man and I would say he was young except that once I knew a Japanese forty-five years old who I thought well under thirty. He was carrying a large paper bag which obscured part of his face, I could not be sure. If I had to say, I would guess that it was Bruce Ching."

"Did you see the man at all, Crane?"

"No, sir. I was flying the plane. Sam had the binoculars."

"We'll assume it was Bruce Ching, and that they were in a hurry about something and started the interviews in the car. Now the question is, can we assume that Doctor Li Kun is in that oil camp?"

Sam thought about it a second. "It is reasonable. It was our assumption that they would leave the country together and we have no reason to believe otherwise."

I interrupted the dialogue. "Am I supposed to know what you're talking about? Because I don't. Who are Bruce Ching and Li Kun?"

Shearing looked at me intently, took a deep drag from his Camel and looked at me again. "It might be sensible to tell you," he decided. "We may need your advice before the night is over." He scratched his head, took another puff. "Bruce Ching is an American-born Chinese. A very brilliant young man. He was at Cal Tech, where he learned a lot about physics, specializing in rockets. After that he was at the Rand Corporation where he became an expert on defense against ballistic missiles. When he had learned enough about it, he defected to China. You understand, he had a top-secret clearance. There was no reason to suspect him, or at least the Bureau detected none.'' He looked around. ''Peters, can you make coffee in this thing?''

''Yes, sir, I'll put on a pot.''

''Thanks. Dr. Li Kun is a naturalized American citizen about sixty years old. When the communists took over China, his expressed sentiments were with the Taiwan government. He worked during World War II with Doctor Ch'ien Hsueh-shen, who was also born in China. Have you heard of Ch'ien?''

''No, sir.''

''Not many remember him outside the intelligence professions. Ch'ien took a Ph.D. from MIT in the Thirties, and was director of the rocket section of the U.S. National Defense Scientific Board during the war. We sent him to Europe to study the German rocket program as soon as it was safe. After that he was the chief research analyst for JPL and a professor at Cal Tech. An important man in our defense effort, you will understand. In 1950 he decided to go to China. He got away in 1955, and some important people credit him with the development of Peking's nuclear weapon.'' There wasn't any humor at all in Shearing's smile.

''And this Dr. Li Kun is pulling the same stunt?''

''Precisely. Li Kun has some rather up-to-date knowledge, and our superiors in Washington would just as soon he didn't take it to Peking. Bruce Ching was a student of his, and we know they sent Ching back to the U.S. to get information on the latest developments in ballistic missile interception. It seemed natural that he'd help his old friend get out of the country. We've followed the one to the other, or think we have.''

''Yeah, OK, I get that. But now you've got Ching. He's out there pumping Steen for the information he wants. What's wrong with just going in and getting them? Their little desert hideaway may be great for keeping people from sneaking up on them, but they aren't likely to get away very easily. No place to go."

"We do not know that Dr. Li is there," Sam answered. "We are not even sure of Bruce Ching, although that is a reasonable guess. I would like to get closer with a good telescope, but they have chosen their base carefully. It does not seem possible without alarming them."

"Yeah. OK, I see the problem. I guess there's nothing to do but wait them out, is there?"

Shearing shrugged. "I suppose not. Unfortunately, our people in Mexico are certain that both Ching and Li will show up there quite soon, and elaborate preparations have already been made to get them out of Mexico. If they once get there, intercepting them will be nearly impossible. Maybe I should have sent you down, Sam."

"Perhaps. But they have been very careful there, and we would have to work very fast."

Nick had been listening to us idly. He was wearing the earphones and hush-mike he'd had in Los Angeles. Suddenly he held up a hand for silence, concentrated for a second, and moved the mike aside. "We may have to work fast here, too. The boys out on the road say an airplane just landed in the desert, right where you say that oil camp is."

18

NICK TALKED SOME more, then turned his set off.
"From their description, that's a Piper Cherokee.
About seven hundred miles range. I think we know
why they came out here now."

Nobody else said anything. I nodded. "Yeah.
When you stop to think of it, this is a pretty good
place to bring a plane in and out. Your people in
Mexico were right, they may be headed down for
tonight. Maybe right now. You better go in and get
them, or call the Air Force or something."

Shearing crushed out his cigarette and snarled.
"Goddamn it. OK, we thought they'd use a plane,
but I didn't really think they'd work so fast. Come
on, Sam, make a suggestion."

I couldn't see why my idea about the Air Force was
wrong, but then I wasn't sure why they didn't just go
in and get them anyway. We seemed to have enough
firepower. De la Torres was studying the map
closely.

"They will have to refuel, I think. And it is getting
dark, will be dark soon. Will they fly out immediately?"

He seemed to be asking me as the local expert on

airplanes, which was quite a compliment after my landing. "Well, it's pretty hot out there. They've presumably got the pilot, Ching, Li Kun, Steen, and Hudson, if they're not leaving anybody behind. That plane wasn't meant for more than four passengers, five overloads it pretty good. The only place to take off would be that dirt road, and there's transmission lines across it. . . . Let's see, it faces crosswind, almost downwind. . . . You know, if it was me, I wouldn't try to get out on that short a runway until it cools off quite a lot."

Janie asked the question, although I don't know if any of them knew. "What does the temperature have to do with it, Paul?"

"Air's thinner when it's hot. Twenty degrees can make a lot of difference when you've overloaded your plane on a short runway. Understand, without the check sheets for that plane I'm just guessing, but I think I'd want to wait a while. Why not wait anyway? They'll try to cross the border at night, won't they?"

"It seems reasonable," Shearing decided. "Now the question is, where do we go from here? I can't go in after them. If that's Bruce Ching in there, we want him to get out. To make this mission come off right, Li Kun and Hoorne must not leave the country, and Ching has to get out without it looking like we wanted him to."

I whistled. "That's a tall order. No wonder you don't want the Air Force."

Shearing was still thinking. He puffed away on a cigarette, drank the coffee Peters had put in front of him, went back to the cigarette. We all watched him. While he worked on his problem I wondered why he wanted Ching to get out. Finally he looked at the map again. "OK. Paul, can you land that airplane on the road above them?"

"Archk?" I think that's what I said. It was a

strangled gasp of some kind anyway. "With a hell of a lot of luck, just maybe. That ship's a sailplane, Mr. Shearing. She's got a wingspan of almost sixty feet, a hell of a lot wider than most roads. You saw how sloppy I was getting her down out there with a full runway. Besides, she's out of fuel."

"No, the boys were filling her when I got the maps," Peters said. I gave him my best look, but he didn't melt and run down the cracks in the floor.

"Take Sam up there while there's still enough light to land," Shearing barked. "We'll look for the other end of that road and try to get some reinforcements behind you by car. Go on, get moving. And now you've had practice, make it a decent landing."

"But—but what in hell do we do when we get up there?" I asked. "Not to mention the fact that the chances are we don't get there in one piece."

"Sam can tell you. You have everything you need?"

De la Torres nodded. "In the airplane already." He turned to me. "Señor, I am not anxious to go up with you again, but what else is there? Only you can fly that craft, and do you know of any other way we can get close enough to them to attempt our mission?"

They were all looking at me again, Sam, Nick, Harry Shearing, Peters. But this time they had an added attraction. They had Janie. Then they weren't looking at me anymore, they were starting out of the camper, with Shearing right behind giving last-minute instructions, and I was alone.

There wasn't any trouble getting the ship off the ground. She liked to fly, and we didn't need much of the runway. I was still muttering to myself as we circled over the hills, came in low above the treetops to skim along that ridge, looking for the stupid road.

"If I pile this thing up, they're going to *know*

somebody's up here," I told Sam. "You think of that?"

"What is there to think? If they are alarmed, Shearing will have to do this some other way. But it would be best for all of us if you did not pile it up."

I swiveled around to get a look at him, just in time to see him hide that little half smile of his. OK, if he could play that stiff upper lip routine, so could I. I wonder how many people have done damn fool things because they're more afraid of somebody grinning at them?

It didn't really look so bad when we cruised over the road. Sagebrush and weed grew right up to the edge, but there was clearance, the trees were higher up. The problem was that the road wasn't straight. It ran along the ridge, not really a road anyway but a gravel track. I couldn't see any ruts, but the wiggles in it scared hell out of me. Just as I was about to give up, we came to a stretch that would just barely do it if I worked everything right.

I cruised along, maybe fifty feet high, memorizing the landmarks on the approach, then climbed for altitude. Flying that airplane was a weird experience anyway. With that whisper-quiet engine my hands thought this was a sailplane, not a powered craft. I got up high enough for our turn, staying out of sight of the oil camp below us, and brought her around.

"Who's the patron saint for this kind of stunt?" I asked.

"San Juan Capistrano is supposed to have levitated on several occasions, although he is not the official to whom aviators usually pray," Sam answered promptly.

"Levitation. Well, he's our man, then. This is as close to it as we'll ever come. Besides, we may just need the real thing before we're down. Reserve me a couple of candles for him if we make it, will you?" I got lined up with the approach. "Now. You see that handle on your left? Not the throttle, the other one, the big lever?"

"Yes."

"Get hold of it. When I say 'now,' yank back on it all the way. You got that? But for God's sake don't do it until I say so. *Comprende*?"

"*Sí. Ich verstehe.*"

It took a second for that to register and before I had time to laugh I was too busy. Once again I lined her up, brought her to where I thought we were about a foot over the road, eased her a bit lower. The end of my straight stretch was coming up too fast.

"NOW!"

As Sam hauled on the spoilers, I gave her some throttle, keeping her level. We dropped the last foot to the road, bounced along, slowing rapidly, the feathered prop and brakes doing the job. There was still fifty feet of reasonably straight road ahead of us when we came to a stop.

"We make a good team," Sam grinned. "If you can guarantee that in future you can do that well, I will fly with you anytime."

"Yeah. OK, we're up here. What's on the agenda now?"

He was opening some of the boxes in the plane. The long one that ran through both compartments yielded a pair of scope-mounted rifles, little Winchester lightweight 30-06's, the sporterized models. Another box had two pair of big night glasses and a radio. He handed me a rifle and binoculars, fished around and came up with a box of ammunition. We loaded up and divided the rest of the ammo.

"You are said to be expert in rough country. I am going down that hill to get as close to them as I can. If you would like to come with me, I can use the help."

"Help in what way?"

"The man you know as Hudson. If there is any

trouble, concentrate on him. You have a rifle, and you will get into a hidden position where you can watch their camp.''

"You want me to kill Hudson."

"Well, I do not insist that he be killed. Only that he does not kill me."

"Yeah. The things I do to earn an engineering consulting fee. OK, let's go, Montezuma. Sorry, wrong man. About now we could use Cochise or Mangas Colorados."

"Or Davy Crockett. There is one thing, Señor Crane.''

"For God's sake if we're going to get killed together you can at least call me Paul.''

"Paul. One thing. Bruce Ching must leave the country. Steen Hoorne and Li Kun must not. Leave that to me, and concentrate on Hudson."

"Sure. OK, lead on, Santa Ana." We turned and plunged off the road, headed down toward the oil camp below.

It wasn't really hard going. Everything was dry, but there'd been some strong wind along those hills, so there weren't many dead leaves, and the chaparral had burned off a couple of years before. A lot of it had grown back, of course, but it wasn't too thick except for scattered briars and a spiky sort of bush, all over thorns. There were regular Scots thistles too, but at least there wasn't any of that jumping devil-plant Steen and I ran into on Anacapa.

We headed down the ridge line of the finger jutting out into the desert. There was more cover there, and it figured that their guard in the oil derrick wouldn't be watching that direction as close. He'd be far more interested in cars out on the desert road, especially any that stopped.

By the time we got to where we could just see their camp, the sun was gone behind the Temblors, and the light was fading out fast. We didn't have to worry about reflections from our binoculars.

I didn't recognize the man in the oil derrick, and after some thought Sam assigned him to me to worry about. The instructions were to not alarm them unless we had to, but after that I should keep Hudson and the guard occupied, letting Sam concentrate on the mission. If he saw Li Kun, he would have Shearing create a diversion and the battle would start.

When it got dark enough we worked our way down closer, until I found a position about a hundred yards from their camp. I was on a level with the man in the oil tower, and with the big night glasses I could see him fine. There were electric lights in the main building, but no sign of the airplane. They must have hauled it into another shed, and I tried to pick out which one. I wouldn't want to put a bullet in there and risk knocking out their transportation.

Sam left me and moved around to my right where he could see into the main building. I had to admit he was pretty good, probably better than I was. I knew where to look, but after a few minutes I couldn't see him, and he didn't make any noise. I sat there for an hour, waiting, wondering what comes next. This was the damnedest outfit for not telling me anything.

Of course it figured. I wasn't really one of their little band of brothers. More like a brother-in-law, say. The rest of them would have been briefed long ago, and there'd been little time to clue me in on everything. The real puzzle was why they were letting Ching go. After the trouble we'd taken to authenticate Steen, it had to be what he was giving him. I wondered if big lasers exploded, killing everyone in the laboratory, if you built them wrong. Or maybe there were some super-expensive lines of research that didn't pan out, but by changing the results a little they could look like just the thing to do, draining off Chinese talent in wrong directions. I remembered somebody once telling me that we had about five dif-

ferent approaches to the atomic bomb during World
War II, and if any enemy agent had just managed to
tell the Germans which lines were not working, Hitler
would have had the bomb before we did by concentrating all his effort on the one that did. Techno-
logical warfare is pretty complex, and it had to be
something like that, I'd never know what.

All the time I waited I was watching their man in
the oil tower. Suddenly he stopped sweeping his binoculars across the desert, concentrated on a spot a
mile or so away. I looked over to see what he was
searching for but couldn't see a thing. I had con-
cluded he was hunting coyotes when there were several shots out there.

Car lights came on out at the blacktop road, and
there was more gunfire. Somebody must have tried to
force his way up the road, probably Shearing's men.
Sam would know, but he had the only radio.

Men came boiling out of the camp buildings below. Two of them went into the shed, and a few seconds later I saw a low-winged single-engine airplane
being pushed out onto the dirt road. More people
came out of the buildings, moving too fast for me to
recognize from that distance.

Off to my right there was a rifle shot, and one of
the men near the plane went down. The guy in the oil
tower turned toward the flash, firing a little automatic weapon, some kind of carbine. I shot at him,
missed, worked the bolt and fired again. I thought
I'd hit him that time, but I hadn't killed him. He
turned on me, sprayed the area around me. I heard
the swish of the bullets, felt a couple of pieces of
chaparral fall on my back where they'd been clipped
off above me. I steadied the rifle, got a good picture
of him in the scope, and knocked him out of the
tower with my third shot. Then I turned the scope
back onto the group around the plane.

Hudson was hauling on a smaller man kneeling on

the ground. There was a body stretched out there, an older Oriental man I thought, and this guy seemed to want to stay with him, while Hudson was pulling him away. Hudson was my target, and I got him in the sights but I couldn't risk a shot at him for fear of hitting the other guy, who might have been the Ching we were so concerned about.

The engine started on the plane, and Hudson got his man away from the body, heaved him into the aircraft. As he did, a tall man ran out of the shed, got to the airplane and started to climb onto the wing. From the height and the way he ran, I knew him. It had to be Steen Hoorne.

Hudson stood out of his way, turned toward the hills and fired a couple of shots with a pistol, which seemed pretty stupid since he didn't have much to shoot at. The shots were answered, though. De la Torres' rifle barked again, and Steen fell backwards out of the plane, stretched out on the ground under the wing. Somebody inside flashed a light on him for a second, and with the full nine power of the variable scope I didn't have any trouble at all seeing the big bloodstain spreading across his shirt. I remembered how Shearing had put it. Li Kun and Hoorne must stay here. Somehow I didn't think Sam had been shooting at Hudson at all.

19

I REMEMBERED THAT Hudson was supposed to be my
assignment and I looked for him in the sights. I
wanted to shoot somebody. I would have preferred
Sam de la Torres, but Hudson would do, only I
couldn't find him. They'd closed the door of the
plane from the inside, maybe he'd climbed aboard
while I was still looking at Steen's body. De la Torres
had plenty of opportunity to shoot Hudson if he
really wanted him, but I didn't think he'd hit him,
there weren't any bodies showing. If he'd shot at the
man, he'd have got him, I suppose. He'd already
proved he knew how to shoot. There were two bodies
out there to prove it, and one of them was my friend.

The little Piper taxied away fast, rolled down the
dirt track without a runup, which is bad procedure,
but under the circumstances the pilot didn't have
much choice. I didn't envy him taking off in the dark
with those transmission lines down there somewhere.
I put a couple of rounds out in their general direction
for effect, we wouldn't want them to think they were
supposed to get away. Now that he'd been killed for
it that would be a hell of a waste of a good sailor.

The plane roared off down the road, bounced, hit

again, and was airborne, flying over the running gun battle still in progress farther off in the desert. It climbed steeply, almost at its stall angle, the pilot obviously unsure of those transmission lines and determined to get over them. He kept on climbing long after he'd got enough altitude, and the sound of the engines died away in the night. There didn't seem to be anyone left alive in the oil camp.

I waited a couple of minutes, then began to work my way down there. With all that blood there wasn't much chance that Steen was alive, but if I could I wanted to help. On the way I tried to think what I might do, but the first aid courses I'd taken didn't include much about chest wounds. Back in OCS we had some drill on that, but I couldn't remember much about it. I'd slept through most of the classes.

I was thinking about that instead of what I was doing, and I was almost to the sheds when I saw I wasn't alone. A little short guy was coming out of the brush fast, a rifle across his chest, big binoculars flapping at his side. When he got to the lighted area a burst from one of those automatic carbines cut him down, and he rolled over, flopping around in the dirt. Hudson came out of the shed fast, running hunched over, almost stumbling over Steen's body, headed out into the brush where Sam had been. I realized that the man with the rifle must have been de la Torres.

I whipped off a shot at Hudson, but the light was bad and I had to fire across the barrel without sights. Then I got down to the ground, worked the control on the scope to get back to about four power and a wider field of vision. Hudson reached the edge of the brush and fired another burst in my general direction, but he wasn't even close.

We were back to stalking games again, but I had to work around the lighted area of the sheds, and by the time I got to the chaparral he'd moved on up the hill

to another position. Neither one of us was very quiet
about it. You can't be when you're in a hurry.

I had the more accurate weapon, but his could
spray down an area, and the light was too poor for
good shooting anyway. I decided my best chance was
to outdistance him, get above him and force him
back down onto the desert where Shearing's people
could take him. Crouching as low as I could, I
dashed up a draw, running for altitude and the hell
with the noise, anything to outdistance him.

He could see my plan, but before he decided to
make a race of it he fired another burst at me. I heard
the bullets whipping around me, but he must have
been moving the rifle to try for area shooting. Nothing hit me. Then he started to run up, but he wasn't
making much progress. I began to wonder if my snap
shot hadn't hit him after all. Anyway, it was simple
enough to get ahead of him, and once above him I
got a position and scanned through the brush, trying
for a clear shot. He'd gone to ground.

There was a car moving up the road toward us
now, playing a big searchlight out ahead of it. Whoever it was didn't care about being seen. I listened
and realized the battle was over out that way, which
had to mean that Shearing's people had won. At least
I hoped it meant that, but actually I had no way of
knowing how many troops were involved from either
side. I wondered about Janie, and if Shearing used
the girls for an assault.

At the moment I was in a pretty good position
either way, able to keep Hudson pinned down below
me, or run like hell to get away if it turned out the
friends of suffering Asia had knocked off Shearing's
clean-cut fine upstanding American boys. At the moment I didn't give much of a damn. Maybe it was important to keep Steen from being carried off to Peking, but they could have found another way. Sam de
la Torres must have intended this all along, and I

hated his guts. I wondered if he was still alive down there. The last time I'd seen him he was still moving.

The car got closer, and there was another burst from that damn little spitgun down below me. The guy had got himself into a depression where I couldn't see him, and I stood, getting careful aim, waiting for him to show himself again. The lights went out in the car, and people were piling out of it, diving onto the road, with another burst from that carbine to keep them moving. At that range he couldn't hope for accuracy, but if you spray an area long enough you'll hit someone.

I fired, worked the bolt, fired again. There wasn't any chance of hitting him, but it might keep him busy, and if I couldn't see him to shoot at, he had the same problem. He realized it and moved out of his draw, spraying down the general area around me, and I lined up the sights on his chest, began to squeeze off the round. Suddenly there wasn't any target to shoot at, and I heard the sound of a rifle from below us. We'd both forgotten Sam de la Torres. He might be a rotten swine, but he sure as hell could shoot. Hudson rolled down the hillside with half his head blown off.

The camp was crawling with people when I got back down to it. Peters and a guy I didn't know had a group of handcuffed prisoners herded into the shed where they'd kept the plane. Two other men in white coats had bundled Steen's body onto a stretcher, covered his face with a blanket and were carrying him off to an ambulance that drove up with four or five other cars. A highway patrol cruiser and two Kern County sheriff's cars pulled up behind me, and some other character identified himself to them as the FBI special agent in charge here.

There were more medics working on Sam de la Torres, putting tourniquets around both of his legs. He seemed to have taken one in each thigh, maybe more, and I wondered how he'd been able to roll around and work the rifle. Well, I never thought the little guy didn't have guts. Janie was in the circle around him, and I got to them just in time to see one of the medics slip him a hypodermic. De la Torres had the little smile I'd seen before, but it was an effort to keep it there.

"Hold it right there!" somebody shouted. "You! Who the hell are you?" Someone grabbed me by the shoulder and whirled me around. A uniformed deputy took the rifle I was carrying while another frisked me, found the Luger and looked triumphant. "Trying to act like one of us," he said. "Now just who the hell are you, with this foreign gun?"

"Don't say anything," Janie told me. "Bring him over here, officer."

They frog-marched me around the building, and a minute later Nick joined us. "He's an undercover man for us," Nick told the deputies. "I didn't want the prisoners to get a look at him. It's all right, officer, give him his gun back."

The cop looked like he was parting with his last friend, but he handed over the Luger. The other one started to offer me the rifle, but I shook my head. "The Luger's mine. I don't need that goddamn thing." The cops stepped back, but they weren't leaving a desperate criminal like me unwatched. They still didn't believe Nick, thought they had a good arrest.

"It all—all worked fine," Janie said. "The whole mission." She glanced around at the policemen. "Perfectly."

I could see them loading Steen's body into the ambulance. Another group had Sam on a stretcher. Whatever they'd shot him full of put him out, but he still had his little smile. Janie saw where I was looking and said, "His legs are pretty bad, but they think they can save them. He'll limp on his left one, but. . . ."

"Too goddamn bad it didn't cripple him," I said. "OK, so it worked perfectly. Now leave me alone."

The cops edged in closer, and the one who thought he'd caught a spy put his hand on his pistol. They were just kids, I saw. You couldn't blame them. A Kern County deputy wasn't likely to see a pitched battle in his lifetime, and never spies and secret service men. Janie gave me a hurt look, put her hand on my shoulder.

I drew away. "Just let me alone," I said. "Look, there's a goddamn airplane up on the ridge. I'll go fly it out, take it to Santa Monica. Soon as it's light." I turned away from them and headed for the hill. It would be a long climb in the dark, something to do to keep from thinking about a big Norwegian character who could sit up on deck with the tiller all night in a gale.

"Paul, wait . . . Paul!" Janie called.

"There's nothing to wait for. Like you said, it was a perfect mission. Now let me alone, goddamn it." I started up the hill. She wanted to come after me, but Nick held her back.

20

THE WATER WAS clear and warm, and I had the anchorage all to myself, a little cove halfway up Catalina Island where I could swim ashore or just lie around on deck in the sun. At night I could hear the goats calling each other, and sometimes in the early morning the hills would be alive with them. I'd been there a couple of days and it was time to move on, but I wasn't sure where to go. It would be a long cruise back up to Seattle and I didn't have anybody to steer through the nights. Part of the way I could hop from harbor to harbor, but after I got out of Southern California it was a long way between safe anchorages. I could worry about that later.

The tide rolled in, slipping through the rocks, reminding me of something with its rushing sound, but I didn't want to remember what. I kept telling myself I was a fool, I ought to at least let the girl say something, but what would she say? She was right, it was a perfect mission. Probably Steen volunteered for it, knowing perfectly well what might happen. They couldn't let him out of the country alive, and given the choice maybe I'd rather have a clean bullet through the back than years in a Chinese prison having everything I knew dredged out of me. Maybe we saved the country for a few years, but that was something else I didn't want to think about. Not right then.

The big Chris-Craft shattered the peaceful moment I'd had, the twin engines driving the goats off into the hills and sending the petrels screaming off into the air. I didn't have to look up to know who was calling me from the deck.

"How was Washington? Happy?" I asked him.

"Washington was fine. I had a hell of a job finding you, Crane. The Coast Guard's been looking for two days." I remembered the white helicopter that flew over earlier in the morning, circled and took another look at me before heading north toward L.A. "Get over here, I've got some people who want to see you."

I started to tell him to go to hell, but I couldn't really get mad at Shearing. He'd always made it plain that winning the war took first place over everything else. I didn't like him, but he wasn't easy to hate either.

The dinghy was tied alongside, and it didn't take long to cross over and climb aboard the Chris-Craft. Peters was out on the bow letting go the anchor, and Shearing was in the cockpit with a tall glass which he handed me. "Drink this, you'll need it."

I sniffed at it, started to set it down, but that was ridiculous. If they wanted to slip me something, they'd do it with a needle anyway. I took a long swig and almost gagged. "Straight gin? Good God, what for?"

"Come below."

Janie and Steen Hoorne were sitting at the big dinette table. I looked from one to the other, looked again, and took another slug of the gin. Steen was grinning like an idiot. "Sorry, skipper, but I'm officially dead. Can't even be seen on deck until the surgeons get through with my face. Come on, man, it's me.''

"Yeah.'' I didn't know what to say, and I couldn't look at Janie.

"They tell me you were upset, skipper. Look, there wasn't anything they could do. There were prisoners, Bureau men, those local cops all around, nobody could explain it to you.''

"I tried,'' Janie said. "Oh, Paul, I tried, but you wouldn't listen, darling. You went storming up that mountain without a word, and there wasn't a thing I could do.''

"Yeah.'' I seemed to be repeating myself. "How'd it work?'' I asked him. "You were covered with blood, I saw it.''

"My cough medicine. There was a little capsule in it, when I crushed it in the bottle it turned it all red. Looks just like blood. When the shooting started, I insisted they take me with them to Mexico or wherever they were going, so they'd think I was as worried about being caught as they were. Had to make them believe I was genuine to the last. I said I'd rather work for them than be in jail. Then Sam put a bullet close to me, I poured the goop across my chest, and died. It was up to you people to keep them from getting close to the body.''

Shearing took the helmsman's seat. "Didn't you think there was something odd about a man as experienced as Sam de la Torres getting caught so easily? He saw Hudson going over to examine Hoorne, so he showed himself and damn near got killed.''

I took a deep breath. "How—how is he? Janie said . . .''

"He'll be all right,'' Janie answered. "They've got the bone reassembled with silver pins. He says you owe San Capistrano some candles, and you can light one for him if you feel like it.''

"I will. By God, I will."

"We lost another man down by the road," Shearing added. "But it worked. The chase planes played games with them all the way to the Mexican border. Ching's convinced he got the real goods from Hoorne and escaped by a hair."

"What was it?" I asked. "Something to sabotage their anti-missile effort?"

There was a long silence. Shearing took out another Camel, examined it carefully, finally nodded. "You've earned the right to know. No, it was perfectly genuine information. Look, we haven't kept you in the dark for the fun of it. During most of the assignment you were in an exposed position. Somebody could have got hold of you and made you talk, and the less you knew, the better for everybody including you. Then when things broke they happened pretty fast, there wasn't time."

"But—" I took a slug of the gin and started over. "But why did you want them to have the genuine information? And if it was genuine, why go to all this trouble to make them think they stole it?"

"Have you read the newspaper accounts?"

"No. I saw some of the headlines, but I didn't feel like reading them."

"Well, the reporters have the official version. No matter how hard anyone checks, no matter who does the checking, they'll get the same story unless one of us talks. The FBI has brilliantly foiled an attempt to smuggle Dr. Steen Hoorne and Dr. Li Kun out of the country. Unfortunately, both turncoats were killed in the attempt to prevent their escape. Some minor Chinese agents got away to Mexico in a light plane, but no one is worrying about them." He took a deep drag on his Camel. "So, they think they got the information from Hoorne and we don't know it. We don't mind if they have a good antimissile system. Maybe they'll use it against the Russians. But it does help our strategic flyboys to know just what kind of antimissile system the Chinese are investing their money in. They got real information, and when they check it out, it will work. I'm not enough of a physicist to know just what loopholes there are in the system Hoorne sold them, but I gather there are some if you know precisely where to look.''

"I see." I really did see, at least enough to know it made sense. I'd put away enough of the gin to be able to face them now. "I'm sorry, Janie. I must have been—well, I'm sorry."

"It's all right." She smiled at me, fingering her hornrims, then took them off.

"What happens now?" I asked.

"That's one of our problems," Shearing said. "The Bureau is still convinced you had something to do with Hoorne, although you're in no trouble, they can't prove anything. The people in the Bureau who know you've worked with us in the past can't say anything, though, and the others will have it in for you. I wouldn't try to get a security clearance, and they may go to some of your customers. When they think they've caught a traitor and can't make it stick, some of the boys get over-enthusiastic. There's no way to turn them off without destroying everything we've gained."

I thought about that one for a while, and he went on. "We'll see you don't starve. By the way, Vallery turned up in Bakersfield, and we're honoring the agreement you made with Beverly. He and the Henderson girl will be released after they've told my people everything they know about Information Associates' customers. I already told you about Prufro. And, let's see, Steen gets a new face, his fingerprints won't need changing because we changed the cards on file for him before this ever started. With a new identity, he . . . well, we've got something for him to do. Janie was too close to this, she'll lose her job at the bank and we'll have to put her on a new assignment. I can't really tell you what my people are doing, Paul, as long as you want no part of us.''

"Yeah. Well, I suppose one of your corporations will keep me out of the poorhouse.''

"Sure. We could also find something else for you to do, if you're interested.''

Peters was messing around on the deck above us, making a clatter. The only other sound was the gentle surf on the rocky beach. After a minute of that, Shearing nodded. "You think about it. Janie, did you have something to say?''

"I've got a couple of weeks leave coming . . . Paul, I brought my things. You said you wanted to show me the islands, will you?''

I took her hand for a second. "Sure. Get your stuff.'' She went below to the forecabin, and I shook hands with Steen. "I hope I recognize you next time I see you, Iron Man. I'd like to have you along for this cruise, but I don't suppose Mr. Shearing wants to take any chances.''

Steen grinned. "No. And I don't think you want another crewman along anyway, skipper. We'll sail again one of these days.'' Janie came up with a sea bag. She stowed her glasses in her purse and looked at me expectantly. Steen's grin was broader, and he clapped me on the shoulder. "Right now, you've got all the crew you need, skipper.''

He was right, of course. I looked at the chart inlaid on the dinette table. Mission San Capistrano wasn't far down the coast, and there was a good harbor near it. "Yeah. I think I'll go down and light those candles in San Juan's home territory.''